BAG a boyfriend

READY, SET, ARGUE!

Bag a Boyfriend

Frances Duncan

Published by Frances Duncan, 2023

This is a work of fiction. Similarities to real people, places, or events are entirely coincidental. Similarities to Jane Austen's Pride and Prejudice are to be expected.

BAG A BOYFRIEND

First edition 14 January 2023

Written and published by Frances Duncan

Also by Frances Duncan

Alison's the Sensible One
Beautiful Abomination
The State of my Life
A Little Bit Austen
Bag a Boyfriend

Watch for more at https://francesduncandoes.com.

Teaser

"When she pulls away *kiss* her."

Lizzy felt Charles stiffen in her embrace at the tinny voice coming from his ear piece. If her head hadn't been resting on his shoulder, she doubted she would have heard it. The manipulation wasn't unexpected, nor was it welcome – but to hell with it, she'd got this far, she might as well go for the win. She took pity on Charles, who was a sweet guy after all – she didn't want to see him in trouble with whoever was feeding him instructions.

Lizzy tilted her head so she'd brush along Charles' cheek as she moved back from him, a split-second decision or this hug would last too long and become awkward. She lingered at his mouth for a beat and waited for him to make the move.

He didn't.

Lizzy gritted her teeth, pushed down her frustration, and fluttered her eyelashes before making the move herself, as he obviously wasn't going to, by pressing her lips to his. Thankfully Charles didn't move away but shuffled her slightly around, away from the camera. Smart man, he wanted people to make up their own minds about the kiss, so that hundreds, possibly thousands, of viewers could imagine it to be as passionate as they desired and not see the reality of two friends, lips together, not moving – though hers did pull into a slight smile at his chivalrous efforts.

Just as she'd suspected, there were no sparks. The sense of disappointment that accompanied this realisation surprised her. Charles was a great guy by all appearances, but not for her.

They broke apart and Lizzy remembered to smile up into his face, one beat, two, then she backed away slowly. She managed not to wipe her mouth though every fibre in her being was telling her to. The camera would catch it, as it caught everything, and next thing she knew she'd be the villain of the piece.

That move had probably secured her a bag at the next ceremony, the ludicrous replacement for the bachelor's rose in the *Bag a Boyfriend* franchise. Her collection of locally made designer handbags was growing. A clutch for surviving day one, and a handbag the next day; there was a rumour amongst the girls that a full set of luggage was waiting at the end of the show, along with Charles.

What more could they expect from "a cheap provincial version of *The Bachelor* on steroids" as Caroline had put it – more focussed on highlighting local businesses than dates with six girls over five days. It was spearheaded by "some washed up TV producer who got downgraded to regional TV because he was – *ahem* – fraternising."

"What's fraternising?" Lydia had asked.

"Think of another word that starts with F," Caroline said. "It's a lot shorter."

Lydia laughed while Lizzy wondered how Caroline knew so much. Could she be a plant by the production, here to stir up drama? Based on the way she treated the other contestants it seemed likely; based on the way she treated the crew, it didn't.

Several local businesses had got together with the local TV channel and radio station to produce this debacle. Every single thing was sponsored. Local restaurants, local activities for the dates, and the local travel place had provided a weekend getaway for the "winners". It stretched across a week, with five full days of filming. The women were sequestered together while Charles materialised to take them each in turn on a date. In the evenings they'd go about their regular lives, giving radio interviews and promotions for the sponsors, if there was anything of the evening left. So far, Lizzy had been too exhausted from the day to do anything other than go directly to bed.

It was ridiculous to imagine a week was enough time to get to know someone, though Lizzy admitted she already had a good read on Charles.

"Thank you for a lovely afternoon," she said simply to him; any gushing could be misinterpreted too.

"Thank–thank *you*," Charles said, still a little thrown by the kiss she guessed. "Let me walk you to your car."

He reached for her hand – whether this was of his own volition, or prompted by the voice in his ear, she accepted the gesture. The camera followed them as they wandered down the picturesque street, strewn with cherry blossoms from the trees above; a lovely couple in the spring, walking with clasped hands. What a shame it was all a farce.

Lizzy could almost feel the second the cameras were off them and let herself relax a little, the tension easing from her shoulders. They were still wearing microphones so she couldn't totally relax, although she was more than ready to tease Charles about saving him from the big bad overlord who wanted him to molest innocent women. It was a shame – Charles was a nice guy, if a little shy, and Lizzy wouldn't have minded getting to know him better. Only as friends though, she was quick to remind herself, as if Charles could hear her thoughts.

Charles opened the door of the car for her; he was always a gentleman, even off camera, and she slid into the cool interior. She knew she couldn't fully unwind until she was back at the ladies suite – they were careful to never utter the word "bachelorette", or indeed "bachelor", for fear of being sued by the big American company that owned the rights. Here's hoping they weren't sued for the rest of the stolen format.

Pre-production

"Ladies. Ladies!" The assistant director had to call them to attention twice as they were all chatting. "Welcome to your week of *Bag a Boyfriend*." He paused, either to let this sink in or possibly because he was waiting for whoops of joy.

Lizzy glanced around at the other women who, like her, just looked tired.

"One of you will be leaving here with a boyfriend and the rest of you will be leaving with a selection of designer bags. All of you will receive some level of fame." He paused again as though he expected gasps; none of them even raised an eyebrow. Lizzy didn't relish the idea of being recognised in the street for doing this.

Lizzy bit back a yawn. It was far too early in the morning to be up, let alone standing in a ballroom with an overzealous AD. But for the week the show filmed she'd be up before the sun to make her call time, even though she'd be spending most of the day waiting around while "the boyfriend" was on dates with other women. Perhaps she could nap while the cameras were off with them. Her boss, Denny, had forbidden her from taking a laptop, insisting she "embrace the experience", so it wasn't like she had anything else to do. But she worried what state the office would be in when she got back. Denny relied on her for everything. By the end of the week, if she made it that far, she was going to be exhausted by sheer boredom.

The AD was still talking. "I will be your wrangler. If you have any questions you ask me or you ask one of my assistants who will get me for you. Do not talk to other members of the crew, do not talk to the boyfriend off camera, try to keep all interactions amongst yourselves on camera. The camera is king – we want it to capture as much as it can, ok?"

Then why the hell wasn't this being filmed?

There were murmurs and nods from the other women. Lizzy wanted to tell them to go to hell, and get the hell out of there; she didn't like being told what to do. But it was too late, she'd signed up for this, there was a contract in place. Although, technically, this was her mother's fault.

**

"You've got to be kidding me, Mum," Lizzy said, exasperated. "You want me to go on reality TV to meet a guy?"

Her mother had pulled some stunts in the past – the last guy she'd been set up with came to mind – but never anything like this, she must be really desperate for grandchildren. Lizzy kicked herself for not realising her mother had an ulterior motive when she was invited over for coffee. But reality TV was a new low, one she never imagined her mother sinking to.

"You're beautiful enough to get on and you never know," her mother shrugged, "you could meet the guy of your dreams."

Lizzy shook her head.

"Uh-uh, you cannot flatter me into doing this." She pointed a finger at her own chest. "I may be beautiful but I'm smart too. *Too* smart to do something like this. The only way I'm getting involved in *Bag a Boyfriend* is with a bag over my head...cos I'm being forced too...obviously."

Her mother pulled a face and looked away, suddenly intent on inspecting the kitchen wall.

Lizzy sighed with resignation. "You've already sent in my application, haven't you?"

"Well, I expected some level of resistance..." her voice trailed away apologetically; she was still unable to meet Lizzy's eye. Her fingers traced patterns on the surface of the wooden table.

"You are incorrigible." But Lizzy couldn't help but smile. After all, her mother was a good source of hilarity. "Why are you doing this?" If it was just for grandchildren, she could turn her mother down flat. Not for the first time, she wished for siblings to dilute her mother's attention.

"They went around all the local businesses, asking for sponsors, asking for suggestions for participants and I thought, well... I thought why not do both at once?"

"You're sponsoring the show?"

"Not exactly, I'm sponsoring you. If you get on the show, which I know you will, because you are so lovely and I can't understand why some deserving guy hasn't snapped you up already, they'll give my shop free advertising and you know how hard things have been lately and I thought I was doing something great for my store and for you all in one go." She spoke quickly, as though afraid Lizzy would interrupt before she came to the end of her justification.

Her mother owned a little craft store which also sold home-made fudge – the real money earner. The past year had been hard on business, with her mother the only employee that survived. Lizzy knew how much it meant; quite apart from it being her mother's livelihood, it was her life. She was friends with her customers and liked to meddle in their lives just as much as her daughter's.

"All you ever do is work, you don't date. I thought it might be good for you. *Please*, Lizzy?"

Years of bowing to her mother's wants, the habits of trying to please her, warred with her hard-won adult independence. She rounded the table and hugged her Mum, old habits die hard. She patted her mother's blonde hair, now shot with silver. After all her mother had done for her Lizzy could do this. She had raised Lizzy alone, a fact that was sure to come up if Lizzy protested too hard. There were only vague memories of her parents yelling at each other. Taking in her mother's familiar scent, lanolin from wool and sugar from fudge, Lizzy wondered if this could actually lead to something great, perhaps she *could* meet the man of her dreams – and fulfil her mother's dreams too. Ha, no. She was doing this for her mother, and her mother's business, that was all. Her mother was right, with work she had no time for dating.

At first, Lizzy had been sure she wouldn't get in; the conversation in her mother's kitchen would be the end of it, she'd never hear from the production company. But she did. What followed was a barrage of tests and interviews including, she was disturbed to find, an STI and pregnancy test.

"Is this really necessary?" she asked the, thankfully female, doctor.

"If you want to do the show," the doctor replied, one hand on the curtain. "It's in your contract."

Lizzy nodded in resignation and the woman pulled the curtain shut. Apparently this was what constituted a 'full and thorough background check'. She slid her underwear off then balled it in her hand and lay on the bed, pulling the provided sheet across her knees.

"Ready," she called, though she wasn't.

I guess they don't want any surprises, Lizzy mused though she bristled at the intrusion. Still, it could be worse – at least there wasn't going to be a camera in there along with the speculum. She could just imagine this splashed all over the papers – "*Compare Contestants Vaginas.*" It made her feel sick just thinking about it – or that could be the speculum between her thighs.

"Just try to relax." Like that was easy to do on a hard bed in a sterile environment with someone inspecting your private parts, the plastic sheet not protecting your modesty. Honestly, what was the point when they just looked under it?

There was a cracking noise as the instrument was widened. Yes, that was definitely making her nauseous. She knew she was going to have a stomach ache after, like last time she had a smear test.

The worst bit was over and the doctor started to remove the apparatus. "I need you to relax," she repeated, then added, "Your muscles are clenching it and I can't get it out."

Lizzy was mortified but took deep breaths, staring at the picture of a forest on the ceiling – surely placed there for moments like these – and willed her internal muscles to let the damn thing go. She blew air out as if she was giving birth; she didn't want this to last any longer than necessary.

Completely demoralised Lizzy put her underwear back on and try to prepare herself for the next hoop she had to jump through but the invasive test hadn't put her in the best mood for the interviews. Despite wanting to support her mother, she couldn't help but give sarcastic answers to the questions posed. Maybe, just maybe, they wouldn't like her and she could go home, tell her mother it hadn't worked. And figure out another way to promote the business.

"Do you believe in true love? Do you believe in love at first sight?"

Lizzy stared at the pair of interviewers, they looked young enough to be teenagers. What did they know about love?

"I'm supposed to say yes, aren't I?"

This was reality TV after all, they couldn't honestly expect her to meet someone and form a real relationship in this contracted timeframe, and she told them so. Unfortunately, they lapped up her answers and egged her on; she assumed it was from boredom at the cookie cutter answers they'd been receiving from everyone else.

"Our notes say you were raised by a single mother. Do you think that has any bearing on you being unable to form a lasting relationship?"

Lizzy rolled her eyes, "What is this, Pysch 101?"

She was glad there were no follow up questions about her relationship with her father who she hadn't seen in years.

After the tests and interviews, it felt like an accomplishment to get on the show. She'd already endured that much humiliation she might as well see it through. How bad could it really be?

Production

Day One

The first day started with a haze of tiredness – being shown around the set and meeting her "competitors" whose names she promptly forgot. The production was based in the fanciest hotel in town; the solitary suite was for the competitors, while crew had desks set up in the ballroom. She yawned and nodded along, wondering where the coffee was and whether it was normal for there to be this many people involved in such a small production. After depositing their things in the suite they went down to the ballroom where food and coffee was provided; Lizzy gratefully procured a cup. As she sipped the hot liquid she surveyed the room; catering was tucked in an out of the way corner, crew desks along one wall and in the centre of the room a stage was set surrounded with lights and cameras.

After the brief relief of coffee there was hair and makeup, back in the suite, which was a little bewildering. Lizzy resolutely kept her mouth shut, as she was directed, but it went against her nature to not chat to the sweet girl who introduced herself as Maria. Instead, she stared at her appearance as it became unrecognisable in the mirror, brown lines appeared that were buffed into shadows, her skin seemed to shine. Beautiful, but unrecognisable. What the hell had she gotten herself into?

There were five other women; the most beautiful, and the one who made the most effort to encourage talking, was Jane. She had natural blonde hair – Lizzy knew enough about hair to know this – and soft blue eyes. She could have walked off the page of a magazine. Lizzy had to stop herself staring. How she had never seen Jane around town before? She was hard to miss. Perhaps her mother was right, she did work too much.

"I'm really looking forward to getting to know you this week," Jane said with a bright smile which made Lizzy blush. Jane barely needed any make up but the effect made her look somehow more angelic. If she didn't seem so genuinely sweet she would be easy to hate.

Lizzy smiled back, hoping the caked makeup on her cheeks wouldn't crack. The last time Lizzy had worn a mask like this had been for school when she played a witch in the Scottish play but the camera would be closer, and more unforgiving, than a children's theatre audience.

Jane remembered everyone's names and introduced them to each other as they waited in the hotel ballroom for the main event. Lizzy realised with a jolt that every one of them was white and blonde. If any of them mentioned being a cheerleader she was out of here.

Jane shushed herself as the host appeared, local real estate legend Bill Lucas. His face graced advertisements across town and had dominated the landscape for as long as Lizzy could remember. She couldn't think of a more perfect local "celebrity" to host the show. If she squinted she could see the line where his makeup ended. He was as fake as the format and, like the sponsors, all about self-promotion.

"Tena koutou katoa," he addressed the camera. Lizzy was impressed they'd attempted to include some te reo but cringed at the pronunciation. "Welcome to our inaugural event for the *Bag a Boyfriend* series. I am Bill Lucas of Lucas Realty, proud to serve our community, and your host for *Bag a Boyfriend*. Hosted over five weeks, six local ladies will vie for the attention of the boyfriend and be awarded designer handbags for their efforts. Those who fail to impress will go home empty-handed." He paused as though waiting for an "aw".

"Today we have six lucky ladies," he gestured to where they were lined up, "waiting for their chance to meet our boyfriend, local heart throb, Charles Bingley."

Lizzy frowned, the name rang a bell. Was he one of the guys her mother had set her up with? A thrill of dread ran through her then Charles was pushed into the room to walk across the large open expanse, glancing around uncertainly. Hopefully they didn't capture that on camera. He was a good-looking guy who she still couldn't place; he was the very definition of tall, dark and handsome, but there was something uncertain about him which was a bit of a turn off.

Lizzy noticed a figure slip from the door after Charles and join the crew behind the cameras.

Charles looked like a deer in headlights under the glare of the very real production lights. He valiantly shook hands with Bill, who was far more confident with the cameras, and followed his direction to stand in a particular spot. Away from Bill and next to a table with lurid green clutches grouped on it he didn't look any more comfortable, more like he was steeling himself for something. The colour hadn't been popular since the 90's perhaps it was making a comeback; everything else was. The prominent lighting wasn't doing the bags or the boyfriend any favours.

One by one the women were invited across the floor to introduce themselves to Charles and shake his hand. When it was Lizzy's turn they mentioned her mother's shop in her introduction. Her mother would be pleased; even if she didn't last the day the shop had received the promised promotion. She wondered if it was too early to make a run for it, slide past him out the door.

Charles' hand was warm and soft; she smiled up into his face and finally placed him.

"I think you were a few years ahead of me at high school," she said, not an unexpected occurrence. She traced the features of his face with her eyes; he had aged well from the gangly boy she remembered. "How did you get yourself into this mess?" she asked, then slapped her hand over her mouth.

Muffled snorts came from behind the camera – seasoned professionals were hard to find around here, she guessed. At least she wasn't the only one screwing up.

"I'm friends with the producer," Charles answered with a smile, her blurting had seemed to finally put him at ease. "He talked me into it." He paused, then leaned in to say conspiratorially, "I'm not saying it didn't take quite a bit of talking to convince me."

Her mouth pulled into smile. *And that is how you charm, Ladies and Gentlemen.*

Their allotted time was over and Lizzy walked back to her place. Maybe this wasn't going to be so bad, though it was hard to look at Charles and not see the boy. Still, she remembered him as a friendly, kind sort; it wouldn't be a trial to date him. One of the other women had a business mentioned – Lizzy wondered if her mother had talked her into it too. Then they were ushered off to the ladies' suite where, one by one, they would be whisked away by a runner to go on a date with Charles.

"There's no way they're going to keep her around for long," sneered a tall woman, whom Lizzy thought was named Caroline, when Jane left on the first date. "She's too vanilla."

Lizzy immediately bristled; something about Caroline, the way she looked down her nose at everything around her, made Lizzy itch for a fight. She'd already made herself at home on one of the two couches, stretching her legs out as though unaware there were four other women who might like a seat. She examined one of the pillows critically then threw it over the back of the couch.

"She's right, you know," another woman said softly, almost sympathetically. Lizzy wracked her brain – Charlotte! She joined Lizzy on the couch opposite Caroline. "Jane is beautiful and she'll look great on camera but she won't provide any drama."

Lizzy gave her a weak smile then changed the subject.

"I'm promoting my mother's business. I joked she'd have to kidnap me to do this yet here I am. How did you end up here?"

Charlotte, it turned out, was here for some sort of notoriety. She saw it as good publicity for her accounting business. So, she was here of her own volition. Pushing comparisons with Bill Lucas out of her mind, Lizzy focused on Charlotte, who continued, "I'm plain," she said, "I can't go up against the likes of Jane and win the guy so I might as well get something out of this. I want to promote my business and women run businesses in general too. That's my speciality, my niche in the market."

"Was that rehearsed?" slipped out before Lizzy could stop it.

Charlotte didn't seem to mind though, she smiled. "I've been practising my soundbites for the camera. Might need more practice to sound natural."

"Or less," Lizzy suggested. She wanted to protest that Charlotte wasn't plain, but she had wondered how someone who could so easily fade into the background had been picked for the show. Maria had curled Charlotte's ash blonde hair and added more colour to her cheeks but she was right, she couldn't compete with Jane.

Charlotte's goal was a noble one; the local business community was full of men like Bill Lucas. What sort of deal the show had struck with Charlotte? If it was similar to her mother's, promotion in exchange for participation, then the show had fulfilled their end already and

Charlotte could be the first one out the door. Either that or Charlotte was doing the books for the whole production, but perhaps that could be a conflict of interest – would they care if it was?

"What's your line of work?" Charlotte asked.

"I'm an office manager for a design firm."

"What does that involve?"

"Ordering stationery and coffee, managing contracts, sometimes negotiating them, making sure everyone gets paid – staff and vendors, keeping an eye on billable hours especially with the new designers, sort of mentoring them on how to work in an office environment, making sure we don't over run budgets or timeframes...a little bit of everything."

"That sounds like a lot, almost like you run the place."

"I worry about what's happening without me there this week."

The conversation turned to their accounting system and the workarounds Lizzy had implemented to ensure it met their needs.

The remaining two women were Mary and Lydia, seated at the table and ignoring the rest of the room. They were both good looking, but hard to read. Lydia, who was glued to her phone, had dark roots that flowed into long blonde locks, she had been told off on the tour as she attempted to take pictures of their surroundings. Mary was only interested in her book and had pulled her hair back off her face. Neither made any attempt at conversation. Though, after her initial comment Caroline didn't seem interested in socialising either. Instead, she spent the morning arguing with any crew who came to the suite.

"What do you *mean* there aren't any confessionals?" she screeched indignantly while the crew member tried to shush her – there went the no talking to the crew rule. "Where are all the cameras? Why aren't there cameras in here? This is the best part!"

The crew member said something and Caroline swelled with indignation. "I don't *care* that it's not sponsored," she said loud enough for the whole room to hear. "I need to be on camera. All of this," she swept her arm to include the room, "should be on camera." Lizzy cringed at Caroline's abuse but did nothing to intervene. She couldn't fault Caroline's logic; the women talking, to each other or to the camera, was the most engaging part of those shows. But Lizzy was glad to avoid the facilitated drama.

Jane came back from her date with stars in her eyes, and it was Caroline's turn. She threw them a triumphant look as she followed the runner – who looked justifiably terrified of her – out the door. They weren't even half way through the day and Caroline already had a reputation with the crew.

The day dragged, though Lizzy found she had been correct in her first assessment of Jane – a sweeter woman she had never met. She made room on the couch and even attempted to engage the two women at the table in conversation. Charlotte was lovely too; it was her turn after Lydia, who had reluctantly unglued herself from her phone for her date.

Finally, the second to last date of the day was hers. Lizzy, by this point, was ready for a good nap but rallied to show some enthusiasm. The hired car took her to meet Charles at a local winery.

The heels of her shoes sunk into the grass between the vines but she was glad for the height, without them Charles would have dwarfed her. She ran her fingers along a leaf enjoying the warmth of the late afternoon sun on her back.

"You look happy." Charles smiled at her.

"I don't remember when I last spent any time in the sun and fresh air." Lizzy extracted one heel from the grass to move forward. "Most of my days are in an office, but even there I wear more practical shoes."

Charles chuckled and offered his arm. It might have felt strange, old fashioned, in any other context but somehow it worked.

At the end of the row a tasting session waited for them.

"Isn't drinking in the sun a bad idea?" Lizzy asked before she could stop herself.

"I think this set up is just for us," Charles murmured.

He was articulate and kind, telling her about the various wines, but seemed reluctant once they got to the tasting.

"You first," he motioned with his glass.

Lizzy wasn't keen on spitting while being filmed so she swallowed the wine, keeping to small sips rather than mouthfuls, despite the urging of the crew.

"Scull, scull," the guy holding a large microphone overhead urged while the others nodded along, miming drinking. They were scattered along the heads of the rows, leaning against the posts, watching.

She frowned. She hadn't expected this much interference; it felt like they were trying to get her to say something stupid like she had that morning. Instead, she ignored them, smiled at Charles and kept her chat neutral.

"This one's nice."

Charles took an infinitesimal sip and hummed.

At one point he managed to catch her eye while the camera was pointing elsewhere and rolled his eyes. Perhaps he was finding the whole thing as ridiculous as she was. She bit back a laugh and nodded.

At the end of her first date she didn't feel anything, apart from a tiny twinge of disappointment. Maybe she had started to buy into the whole shtick of the show, and her mother's fantasies, thinking she could really meet the man of her dreams.

After all the waiting around, it was a rush to be primped into an evening gown for the bag ceremony which closed the first day. Lizzy was in the makeup chair with Maria the second she arrived back in the suite. Mary, the bookworm, who had the date after Lizzy, protested the speed at which she was whipped into shape.

The women were grouped together on one side of the large ballroom while Charles stood on the other, next to a table displaying the truly awful clutches the lucky women would be awarded with. The whole thing felt very awkward, lights shining in their eyes and a full crew of people watching their every move from the behind the cameras.

"Action."

Bill Lucas introduced himself – and his realty firm – again, before turning to Charles and asking after his day. Charles stumbled through a sentence or two. Did Bill make him uncomfortable? He didn't have that much trouble on their date. Bill took over, addressing the camera again, dramatically declaring that one woman would be leaving tonight. He stepped aside and the camera focussed on Charles.

Charles opened his mouth but before he was able to say anything Mary stepped forward. Lizzy noticed crew gesturing wildly to ensure the camera followed Mary as she crossed the expanse between them. She walked with her head held high as she approached Charles.

"Um, Mary?" It come out sounding like a question.

"Charles, I had a great time with you today and you've got some great women to choose from." She gestured at the small group of them waiting for their turn on the chopping block, as if she knew anything about them and hadn't spent the whole day ignoring them, absorbed in reading. "But..." Lizzy could swear everyone leaned forward, "I don't think you're my intellectual equal. You're a great guy but I need someone who's more cerebral."

Charles blinked rapidly, his mouth open. He looked more confused than insulted. The sweet boy, perhaps the word cerebral had stumped him. Lizzy pressed her lips together to stop from laughing.

"Ah, Mary, I–I appreciate your honesty," he said in stage voice, then he dropped back to his normal level. "Are you sure you want to go? I was going to give you a bag tonight." His arm narrowly avoided sending the bags flying; Mary placed a hand on the table to steady it.

A giggle escaped from Lizzy and she sensed one of the cameras swivel to face her. Oh no, this was not going well. She schooled her face into a look of neutrality.

Mary shrugged.

Charles just stood there looking at her, shifting uncomfortably. *Say something,* Lizzy urged him silently. *This is your show.*

Time stretched until— "Ok, ok, reshoot," one of the guys behind the camera called; with the lights in her eyes she couldn't see who. A collective breath was released.

So, this was the reality in reality TV.

A short guy with brown hair came up to coach Mary; no, he wasn't exactly short but he was a head shorter than Charles. "This time I want you to say you want someone more intellectual, we can't have you insulting the boyfriend." Then he turned to Charles. "Charles, you say you could really see a future with her but you understand her reasons."

Charles nodded.

Mary returned to her place amongst the women before walking across to Charles again.

It took three more attempts till the production was happy.

She may have been rewarded with an ugly clutch that night but Lizzy wasn't sure the aching feet were worth it.

**

"What do you think of Charlie boy?" Lydia asked as they were changing into their street clothes after Mary's shock exit.

Mary had been rushed out before they were allowed into the ladies' suite – perhaps they didn't want her poisoning their minds with her independent thoughts. Somehow, Lizzy had ended up next to Lydia. Though Lydia wasn't her first choice of companion she was at least making an effort to interact. Perhaps because it was impossible to be on her phone while she was changing.

Lizzy shrugged. "He seems like a nice guy." Too nice perhaps to be on a show like this, a bit like Jane really. She glanced across the room with a smile at the woman she already considered a friend after just one day.

"More like dull," Lydia countered. "He wouldn't do shots with me on our first date."

"Well, he couldn't exactly get drunk when he had three other dates, could he?" She realised now why Charles had been so reluctant to drink, only taking tiny sips, he'd been worried she would try to get him drunk like Lydia. Or maybe Lydia had managed to get a few into him and he was already feeling it.

"He could if he liked to party." Lydia slung her bag over her shoulder and a thought slotted in Lizzy's head – *she's the party girl.* Another thought followed quickly after and everything became clear. *Mary was the brainy girl. Which means Jane is the nice one or maybe the pretty one, Caroline is the bitchy one* – she'd already bitched out one of the crew members – *and I'm...I'm...*

She pondered that one as she pulled her jacket on and waved goodbye to Lydia. How old was the girl anyway? She tidied up the mess Lydia had left behind, hanging her dress and throwing the makeup remover wipes in the bin. No point leaving it for the crew who could get resentful – why piss them off when they had the rest of the week together?

Day Two

Charlotte – the sensible one, Lizzy had decided – was the second to go. Lizzy suspected this was because she didn't "pop" on camera as much as the rest of them. It was true that she was, as she had labelled herself, plain, but Lizzy thought they could have been friends and didn't want her to leave. She hoped Charlotte had had enough time to properly promote her business interests. "Business woman" was a better, more fitting, title than "sensible one."

Had her mother's shop had enough promotion yet? She could be next. Maybe when she got back into the real world she'd see Charlotte's face cropping up around town just like Bill's – instead of Bill's. She would be a good face for accounting in the community, for female-run businesses. A young, fresh face; not an old man in a suit.

If only she knew what the contract had guaranteed.

Based on the looks Charles kept shooting the not-short guy, who nodded and gestured emphatically, it seemed like it was the production's choice to let Charlotte go, rather than his. Lizzy decided that guy must be the boyfriend-handler. Eventually, after the third time shooting the scene, the boyfriend-handler had taken Charles aside, procured an earpiece – after shouting at someone – and Charles had parroted whatever was piped into his ear while Charlotte waited patiently. They had learnt their lesson on the first night when Mary left; this wasn't their show. Now it appeared it wasn't Charles's either.

Charlotte had been philosophical about her exit. For some reason she hadn't been kept from them like Mary had been – maybe only walk-outs were kept from the other contestants.

"You know how this works right?" Charlotte said as they rode the elevator down together after changing into their own clothes. "They keep the most interesting people the longest, but they have to take Charles' interests into account. It's clear he's into Jane so they won't get rid of her. But she's boring. She doesn't show any emotion. They won't like that. So, they'll play up his relationships with everyone else."

When they separated on the street Charlotte told Lizzy to look her up if she wanted to talk to another woman in a male dominated industry.

Lizzy watched her walk away, wishing Caroline had left instead. Caroline was proving to be as bitchy as she had been cast, today she'd attempted to order Lizzy to get her coffee, and Lydia was just too young. But at least Jane was still there. Lizzy smiled and wrapped her arms around herself to combat the chilly night air as she walked to her car.

Day Three

Lizzy reached back for Charles' hand, like it was the most natural thing in the world. A part of her wished she felt electricity racing up her arm at his touch. She caught the eye of his handler, watching from behind the camera. She blinked and asked Charles to repeat himself, trying to ignore that intense gaze. The rest of the crew were careful never to invade their space, to make it appear as if they were alone rather than facing a sea of people. She turned her back to them; a camera followed to ensure her face was still in shot as she looked at Charles, smiled up at him. If it weren't for the invading forces this would be a lovely date.

"There's a Japanese concept," he explained, "called forest bathing. I can't remember the word for it. It's about finding, ah, space, cleansing, fresh air, in nature."

"That sounds lovely. Forest breathing."

"Forest bathing."

"Ah." She noticed one crew member nudge another, they were going to make her look like an idiot.

Charles guided her down the gravel path to a little river where water ran rapidly over rocks.

"I love the sound of it," he said. "I listen to something similar to help me sleep."

"Doesn't it—" she stopped herself from asking if it made him need to pee, that would not go down well. Sure, he'd answer but she didn't know how it would appear to the public. That sadistic bastard following them would likely make them film it again, make her say it as sarcastically as possible, implying she thought *Charles* was the idiot.

"Never mind. It is lovely here." She wondered why they hadn't done activities like white-water rafting but answered her own question as she posed it; everything was sponsored, there were no local white-water rafting outfits to need promotion. She'd prefer more adventurous dates like the big productions had, maybe even sky diving. But that wasn't Charles' style, he'd appear even more uncomfortable.

The crew clustered up the little slope, unable to join them by the river. Later they would capture the river itself without them standing in front of it. The idea of forest bathing was lovely but was it possible when there was so much technology close by?

**

I'm next, Lizzy thought on the drive back to the hotel, *if that kiss didn't save me.*

While the camera had captured panning shots without them they retreated to the car where a second camera had captured their kiss. To be more accurate Lizzy had kissed Charles, following the instructions that he was reluctant to.

But kissing Charles wasn't just to please the whispering overlord; the competition aspect was getting to her. If nothing else, she wanted to beat Caroline.

The weird things crew members said to her, trying to prompt her into sarcasm, made her realise she had been cast as the funny one but she wasn't nearly as amusing as they planned. There was pride in thwarting their efforts to humiliate her, yet she had still kissed him, playing right into their plans.

The boyfriend-handler had been watching closely but his face was like stone when she glanced at him after separating from Charles. Surely it had been him telling Charles to kiss her?

It would be better to leave the final three as the party girl, the bitchy one and the nice one. It's clear who the audience would support but there'd be enough tension; Caroline was a great actress, Charles might have fallen for her act.

"Last date of the day," Caroline greeted Lizzy, as she entered the ladies' suite after her date. "You know what that means."

Caroline was already made up for the bag ceremony, her severe bob perfectly straight as ever, behind her Lizzy could glimpse Lydia getting the final touches which meant they were ready for her.

Lizzy closed her eyes briefly; she needed strength to face Caroline without screaming. "There is no curse, Caroline. The production chooses the order of the dates." It had held true the first two days of production, but could it count as a curse when Mary had chosen to leave?

"Either way, I'd be worried if I were you."

Briefly, as she brushed past Caroline, Lizzy wondered if they did order the dates for who was going home. Caroline would be likely to know, she seemed to know more than the rest of them. She turned, opened her mouth to say something then closed it again. Caroline may not be a mole but she was good at stirring drama, there was no point playing into her hands.

"How did your date go, Lizzy?" Jane asked, breaking into her thoughts. She looked stunning in a deep blue full-length gown.

"Am I late?" Lizzy asked, looking around at them and failing to answer Jane's question. They hadn't had to rush since the first day; fewer people meant more time. "You look beautiful," she said to Jane. Remembering she couldn't be upset at Caroline for being bitchy if she didn't try to include her, she added, "You look good too Caroline." Lydia was too busy on her phone to care.

Caroline patted her platinum blonde hair as she looked in the mirror. "It's not their best work but at least they have something to work with." She had not allowed Maria, the hair and makeup artist, anywhere near her hair, complaining that she'd had it treated before the show.

Lizzy rolled her eyes at Jane who smiled apologetically.

In much shorter time than she could have imagined they were lined up in the ballroom ready to receive bags from Charles. She'd been hurried into her gown in quick time. Maria had told Lizzy that a wedding was expected that evening in the hotel and they had to cut filming short.

"It's not like they could film somewhere else when the hotel is a sponsor and it's not like the hotel could turn down actual paying clients either," she explained.

"Let's hope that Charles remembers his lines then," she'd said to Maria, who had given up trying to protest it was real – just as Lizzy had given up trying not to talk to her.

Today they would go down to the final three and the prize for moving on was a toilet bag. Lizzy tried not to fidget as the host exhibited the bag and its many functions. Waterproof and so many pockets with a little hook to hang it. Was this how Bill showed potential buyers around properties? – "and a second bathroom! Oh my!" Lizzy pressed her lips together to stop herself from laughing out loud.

Finally, the sales pitch was over and it was the girls' turn. An assistant placed three bags on the stand behind Charles.

Come on Charlie boy, choose me. I saved you with that kiss this afternoon.

But the first name called was Caroline, who preened as she accepted the bag from Charles. It looked like he did an evasive manoeuvre to avoid Caroline kissing him smack on the mouth. Caroline was obviously very pleased with herself as she walked back to join the other women.

Maybe Lizzy had miscalculated; her stomach dropped a little, maybe they would get rid of her now that she'd kissed Charles. The handler was close to Charles just out of shot but she couldn't see his face with the lights in her eyes.

"Jane."

Jane hurried forward, eager to receive her hug from Charles. She blushed prettily when he kissed her on the cheek and gazed into his eyes. Charles jumped, pressed his hand to his ear and nodded; the handler threw up his hands in frustration. Charles picked up the bag and placed it in Jane's hands.

"This is for you," he said. "I hope you like it." As though he'd picked it out himself.

They stood staring at each other till the handler cleared his throat, then Jane moved back to her place.

Lizzy maintained her smile while thinking, *oh no, I hope it isn't Jane, Caroline and Lydia as the final three. I was sure they'd keep me.*

Bill stepped forward. "And now we are down to the final two. Charles, you must pick either Lydia or Lizzy to receive this beautiful bag and stay in the competition to win your heart."

Lizzy looked at Lydia and gave her an encouraging smile, though anxiety was swirling in her stomach. Lydia didn't seem too worried.

Charles looked to the handler who nodded at him. So he must be the voice in Charles' ear, it made sense.

"This has been a really hard decision. You're both wonderful, beautiful women." Charles paused and Lizzy wondered whether it was for dramatic effect. "But the person I've chosen to get the last bag is Lizzy."

Relief washed over her. Lizzy heard Jane exhale a breath she must have been holding, and a frustrated noise issue from Caroline, as she walked up to accept her bag and obligatory hug from Charles. She tried to shake off a feeling of elation, like she had somehow won. Charles wasn't a prize. And even if he was, she didn't want to win him!

Bill stepped next to Charles just as Lizzy returned to her place. "I'm sorry Lydia, you did not receive a bag. Your journey to love ends here. Please say your goodbyes."

Lydia gave Lizzy a one-armed hug and a smile, then was enveloped by a quietly crying Jane. Caroline gave her a half-hearted pat on the back. Lydia managed to extract herself from Jane's embrace and bounced over to Charles with her arms open.

"Charlie-boy." Like Caroline, she tried to kiss him on the lips but he avoided this and planted one on her cheek; that was smoother than Lizzy had given him credit for. Lydia took his offered arm to exit the room.

Lizzy released a breath slowly as she watched them walk away. There had been no big scenes and she was safe for another day. She was half impressed with Lydia for not telling Charles off.

"All right," a crew member called to the whole room, "we have a unit on Lydia's exit. That's a wrap for everyone else. Clean up and we'll see you tomorrow."

Lizzy, Jane and Carline were hurried out of their borrowed gowns and back into their normal clothes.

"Of course Lydia left, she was too much of a liability," Caroline said. "It was funny when she tried to get Charles to make out with her but she was trying to get him to speed in the car lent to them and just take off with her. She was pretty persistent."

"How do you know this?"

"I listen," Caroline said with a sniff as she turned away from them and left the room.

"Do you want to grab a late dinner?" Lizzy asked Jane as she pulled on her jeans. "I have issues eating on camera."

"Oh Lizzy, I'm so glad you're still here!" Jane said. "You'll keep me calm through this. I like Caroline but she can't make me laugh like you can." At least she was making someone laugh.

"Let's get some food and you'll feel better. Only two more days to go!"

They collected their belongings, along with the items Caroline had left, and started towards the door. The rest of the room had already been cleaned out, presumably for the upcoming wedding – one of the downsides of the hotel only having one suite.

"Don't remind me," Jane said. "What if he doesn't pick me? I mean, I'll be happy if he picks you, Lizzy."

Lizzy smiled. "But you would rather it was you. I know." Neither of them mentioned Caroline. "Don't worry, I want it to be you too. Though I should tell you, I kissed Charles today."

They stepped into the lift and Lizzy pressed the button for the ground floor.

Jane was less concerned about this than Lizzy thought she would be. "Lydia and Caroline both kissed him on their first dates. Besides, you're supposed to be dating him, why would I mind?"

"Oh, I don't know, because you're in looove with him?"

Jane blushed. "I'm not. Though I do think he's lovely and when he looks at me sometimes I forget that it's reality TV and everything else just melts away and it's me and him...." She trailed off. "I haven't kissed him yet. It just feels wrong to do that on camera, you know?"

"He'd be crazy to pick me over you," Lizzy said with sincerity. Not only was Jane the prettiest of them, she was the kindest too.

They returned the borrowed gowns, shoes and jewellery to the assistant waiting in the lobby.

"Caroline's are in there too," Jane told the harried looking woman, who nodded and noted something on a clipboard.

"I swear I've never worn high heels so often in my life," Lizzy said as she handed them over. "Give me flats any day."

They avoided the hotel restaurant, eager to get out of the building, and settled on a pizza place nearby.

"I can't imagine what Caroline would say if she saw us eating this," Lizzy observed.

"She does have a very nice figure," Jane said diplomatically.

"She is constantly on about the food they offer us. Like she wants to exist on nothing but lettuce! Going on and on about how 'the camera adds ten pounds.' How much is that in kg's anyway?"

Jane looked thoughtful. “Hmm, I think 5kg. So not really much.” She pulled out her phone – she was one of those polite people who didn’t put their phone on the table during dinner – and tapped the screen. “I stand corrected, 4.5kg...ish.”

Lizzy pulled a face. “Barely enough to bother mentioning.”

Jane fiddled with her slice of pizza but didn’t pick it up.

“I’m enjoying my time on the show, getting to know you, getting to know Charles—”

“—*not* getting to know Caroline.” Lizzy added but Jane ignored this.

“—but I do miss the kids. It’s hard to be away from them for so long, they develop so quickly.”

The kids weren’t her own; Jane was a kindergarten teacher. Lizzy smiled, she couldn’t imagine anyone better suited to the role.

“I’m sure they miss you too.” She covered Jane’s hand with her own.

“Oh, the poor babies.” Jane blinked away tears. “I feel so guilty leaving them, even if they do have a reliever, it’s not the same. They know me. They trust me.”

“I bet you’re everyone’s favourite. Eat,” Lizzy said, nodding at the pizza, “and you’ll feel better.”

Obediently Jane took a bite and smiled. “Oooh this is good!” she said around a mouthful, surprising Lizzy into laughter. She briefly wondered at Jane’s surprise – did she not normally eat pizza?

Day Four

The ladies' suite felt much larger with just Lizzy, Jane and Caroline there the next day. At least they couldn't fault Caroline for claiming an entire couch. There was still as many crew as ever in the ballroom. Lizzy idly wondered how it would go if there was an all-out war as she picked over the catering selection at breakfast. The two sides had been carefully kept apart throughout filming, perhaps due to the fraternising the producer had been involved in which had got him downgraded to this job. The crew had the numbers but Lizzy bet Caroline was a dirty fighter. They would be hindered by Jane who would refuse to fight, no matter what the provocation. Lizzy thought she might be able to hold her own against two of the crew – maybe the smaller ones. The thought of kicking the boyfriend-handler made her smile.

But who's side would Charles be on? He was friends with a producer but technically he was talent rather than crew which should put him on the some side as the ladies.

"Lucky last today," Maria said brightly, as Lizzy sat down in the makeup chair sipping her coffee. She could probably take Maria if it came down to it.

The smile Lizzy gave her in return was tired. The early mornings and long days were taking their toll.

"Can you do anything about the bags under my eyes?" she turned her head from side to side, looking at the damage in the mirror. Perhaps she should start napping on the couches.

"Of course. Those are my speciality." She began preparing Lizzy's face for the onslaught of makeup. "Charles will never know you were up all night thinking about him."

Lizzy laughed in response. "How are you so chipper all the time? Aren't you tired with the long days?"

"I get some downtime in the middle, and they don't need to me stay to remove your makeup at the end like some jobs I've worked on. Are you finding it hard?"

Lizzy made a non-committal sound, constantly aware that she shouldn't say too much to anyone for fear of it being taken the wrong way.

"I hear you and Jane went out last night," Maria observed, she'd now moved onto foundation. "Did you have a good time?"

"There really isn't any privacy here, is there?"

"A shoot is a bit incestuous. Sometimes we get caught up in the drama of it all. Do you think Jane's a threat?"

"Jane is..." Lizzy fumbled for the right words in case this was being recorded; she didn't want to say Jane wasn't a threat to anyone in case it was used out of context, "...the loveliest person I've met. I consider her a friend."

"Even though you're dating the same guy?"

"Even though we're dating the same guy," Lizzy replied with a nod.

If Maria had asked about Caroline that would have been a different story.

**

Lizzy had the last date of the day again. She wondered if that meant things wouldn't go well for her in the bag ceremony that evening. So far, she had proven there wasn't a curse but it didn't mean production hadn't allotted her the final date for their own purposes.

Jane hadn't returned from her date by the time Lizzy left so they hadn't had a chance to debrief. Caroline had raved about her date to the room at large even though Lizzy was the only one there.

"How are you feeling, Lizzy?" Charles asked.

They were taking a little cruise on the river in a floating restaurant, chatting while they waited for their meals.

"It's so beautiful here," she said, trying to ignore the ever-hovering cameras. She wondered how they would keep them out of the reflections of the wall to wall glass of the boat. "I never do things like this. Thank you for bringing me."

Charles tilted his head to one side as though he was listening to something, which she supposed he was – the ear bud had become an ever-present fixture. "I meant how are you feeling about this experience? A–about me?"

His hand was resting on the table between them, she covered it with hers remembering doing the same with Jane the night before. It brought a smile to her face.

"I'm-I'm..." What was it the women always said on these shows? "...grateful for the experience, to have this... journey with you." 'Journey' was one of the buzz words. "To have met you and-and Jane," she had to remember Jane, keep her at the forefront for Charles too. But she'd forgotten the others, that would look bad. "And everyone else too." And the sponsors. "There are so many things to do here, so many business that I didn't know about." She barely managed not to slump against her chair in relief. Hopefully that was enough to satisfy his evil overlords.

“I’ve enjoyed my time with you too. You’re quite lovely, you know.”

She blushed. She actually *blushed* at the compliment. Now she was going to look like an idiot to the whole town. Thankfully, the food arrived, a steaming hot stone covered with seafood.

“Don’t touch it,” Charles warned, “use the tongs. I had an unfortunate incident with one of these once.”

They made small talk while they shuffled their food around the stone to cook. When the shrimp had changed colour Charles advised they could start eating.

Lizzy hesitated. “I’d hate to make myself sick because I didn’t cook something properly.” She imagined being caught vomiting, if not by cameras at least by her microphone. She shifted and the power pack bumped against the back of the chair – a constant reminder.

“Ah...let’s risk it?” Charles suggested. “If the shrimp is cooked, the rest should be fine. But if you do get sick I’ll hold your hair back.”

“That’s sweet of you. I’d hate to lose your good opinion. How would you know I hadn’t secretly been sneaking out for shots in between takes and was really vomiting my guts up because I was drunk?” She heard the words come out of her mouth, unable to stop them. Great. She was going to look just great on camera. Would this please the boyfriend-handler?

Charles laughed. Then his expression changed. “Ah...kiss before we get fishy?”

She smiled and leaned forward. It was a brief kiss but it felt important, almost natural. Had it been prompted by the little devil in his ear? Was Charles starting to have feelings for her? She pondered this as she turned her shrimp on the hot stone. He certainly didn’t look at her the way he looked at Jane in the bag ceremonies, but there could be something there. It was impossible to have a real talk with him, what with the microphones, the cameras, and the crew around. It was a little suffocating and claustrophobic.

There had to be a way to let him know that she wasn't interested. Because she wasn't. Right?

Charles picked at his meal, she assumed he'd already been fed on his dates with Caroline and Jane. But she was hungry. So, however uncomfortable she felt eating on camera, she did it – making sure to empty her mouth before directing a remark at Charles. Her mother had drilled into her that speaking with your mouth full wasn't ladylike; advice she normally ignored, because she was too excited to carry on the conversation. But conversation was stilted and things were different when there was a camera poised to take a shot of your gaping maw.

"So, I met your mother yesterday—" Charles began, and Lizzy stopped mid-chew; this could be disastrous, "—she runs the craft store in town. I went there with..." He trailed off uncomfortably, obviously he couldn't talk about one of the other girls on a date with her. "I went there yesterday to sample the fudge."

Lizzy finished chewing and carefully swallowed. "Did you like it?" she asked cautiously. She worried that her mother might have flirted with him, or spent the whole time talking Lizzy up in front of his date.

"The fudge was good, a wide range of varieties, and your mother was...very welcoming." Great, she *had* flirted with him.

"I'm glad you enjoyed it. My mother puts a lot of work into her shop and the crafting community."

They both looked at their plates while Lizzy considered what to say next. She loved her mother but was aware she could come off as ridiculous. She worried how she would appear on camera.

"I–She actually suggested that I come on the show. She even filled out my application form for me...and sent it in before asking me. I'm–I'm glad she did though. It's been a good experience." To her surprise she realised that she wasn't just saying it for the cameras, she genuinely had enjoyed it, despite the early mornings, crushing boredom and intrusive cameras.

This time Charles put his hand over hers, "I'm glad too."

Lizzy felt a smile growing on her face.

**

They were back in the same room with the same fake smiles on their faces as they blinked in the lights. At least, Lizzy and Caroline's were fake; Jane's was probably real. Tonight, Charles would decide his final two.

The bag for tonight was a carry-on suitcase – with wheels that swivelled and a retractable handle – and Lizzy had to bite her lip to stop herself laughing again, as she always did when the bags were presented.

"Light-weight, compact and locally made," Bill completed his spiel. "Tonight there are two of these wonderful bags up for grabs – along with Charles." His voice held innuendo, accompanied by a wink to the camera. "I wouldn't mind one of these babies myself. Now Charles, tonight you will be picking your final two. Who will be going home? Will it be Jane, Lizzy or Caroline?"

Charles looked confused. "Am I–am I meant to tell you now?"

Lizzy snorted. Charles' handler came over to school him about rhetorical questions. Oh no, hopefully they didn't get that on camera – they were likely to pull that piece of footage and pair it against something else. Eventually they were back on track and the two pieces of luggage were wheeled forward.

Jane was the first pick, as Lizzy knew she would be, but then it was down to herself and Caroline.

The host popped up again. "Charles, you have one bag left and two beautiful women. Take your time and make your choice," then he faded into the background.

Lizzy tried not to fidget and kept a smile plastered on her face. If she went home tonight it wouldn't be so bad. Jane was still there, he'd pick her and they'd live happily ever after – or at least happily away from the cameras.

"Lizzy," Charles said finally, and she exhaled.

She walked towards Charles and offered her cheek for a kiss, over his shoulder she locked eyes with his handler. It was impossible to tell if he approved or not. She accepted the bag which she rolled away. Part way back to her position she picked up the bag, snapped the handle into place and carried it. Stifled laughter came from behind the cameras. She'd done it again.

Bill stepped forward. "This is classic Lizzy, she has picked up her suitcase rather than rolling it. And now we have our final two. I'm sorry Caroline, you did not receive a bag. Your journey to love ends here. Please say your goodbyes." He stepped back.

Caroline lightly kissed Lizzy, then Jane, on the cheek and swept forth to receive her goodbye from Charles. Lizzy didn't listen to their exchange, she was too busy clutching Jane's hand and grinning at her.

It had only been a couple of days but the magic of the TV bubble was working, she felt close to Jane and she felt happiness on her behalf. Jane was going to get her man.

Day Five

The final date with Charles was different. They were at the local day spa for a barrage of couples' treatments, starting with a massage. It felt weird to only have a robe saving her from indecent exposure, even if it was covering more than her clothes normally did. She pulled the robe firmly around herself, all the way up to her chin.

"It's ok," Charles reassured her, "they'll go out when we get on the...bed. I mean table. I mean when we need to get ready."

Lizzy smiled. Charles turned to greet their beauty therapists who edged around the camera crew.

"You must be the boyfriend," one said, sticking her hand out.

"I'm Charles," he replied as he tried to extract his hand from hers. "This is Lizzy."

The other therapist shook her hand. "He's *cute*."

Lizzy mumbled something incoherent trying to hear the first therapist who was asking Charles how a guy like him could be single. Her therapist abandoned her to also fawn over Charles.

"It's such an *honour* to be on the show," she gushed, now she had hold of his hand and was equally unwilling to relinquish it.

Lizzy peered through the lights trying to find the handler to see if he could save them from this situation. Charles complimented the beautiful facilities making sure to name drop the spa, he was getting pretty good at this. This seemed to remind the therapists they were at work, one gave brief instructions aimed at Charles with a brief glance at Lizzy then they exited, ushering the crew out with them. It was brief respite, they'd be back to film the treatment.

Lizzy and Charles were alone for the first time.

She shifted her weight from foot to foot. It wasn't like she'd never been naked with a man before, and it wasn't like she was entirely naked beneath the robe either but something about this just felt...wrong. They stood staring at each other for a moment which stretched. Then they both spoke at once.

"I don't mind—"

"I can just—"

They laughed and the tension broke.

"We should be quick about this," Charles said. "We don't want them coming back before we're ready. How about I face the wall while you get on the...bed then when you're ready I'll–I'll have my turn."

Lizzy nodded and he turned. She was grateful to him for taking charge of the situation for once. She whipped off the robe and climbed onto the table, lay down and pulled a towel over her.

"Your turn," she called.

There was a knock at the door.

"We aren't quite ready yet," Charles called.

She heard fabric moving and the table creaking.

"Are you good?" he asked.

"Mmm-hmm."

"We're ready," Charles called.

She didn't know how relaxing the massage was going to be, with cameras aimed at her back and forced awkward conversation, but a free massage was a free massage. She was going to enjoy it as much as she could.

**

It was all about to be over. Finally. The week had started slowly but then sped up and now here she was, ready for the final bag ceremony. Lizzy tried to keep herself from jiggling on the spot. Soon, Charles would pick Jane, they would kiss and it would be the obligatory happy ending. She smirked; perhaps Jane and Charles would go into the ladies' suite upstairs and...no, she stopped that thought and chose not to follow it.

Jane shot her a smile and grasped her hand. Something in Lizzy's stomach clenched. This was it.

As though from a distance Lizzy heard Bill welcome the audience through the camera. He went on his little spiel about the single bag that was to be awarded to the lucky lady tonight. It wasn't the rumoured collection, but a full sized piece of luggage that matched the carry-on from the previous day. The bag was rolled to its place then Charles was welcomed to the stage.

He had adjusted, somewhat, to the lights and the cameras. He still looked like a little boy but now he didn't focus on the floor quite so much, his handler still hovered at his side just out of range of the cameras. How would Charles came across on screen? Hopefully the show wouldn't make fun of him, even though they easily could. Everything he did or said was fodder for a blooper real but if they did that, the whole concept would fall apart.

Lizzy squeezed Jane's hand.

The host was talking to Charles about his "whirlwind" romances but didn't mention the extremely short timeframe, they referred to weeks instead of days. Yet another "reality" of reality TV.

"And now, you are down to the final two. Lizzy," he paused and Lizzy felt everyone's eyes on her, "and Jane. Two more different women you couldn't meet."

They weren't that different, were they? Sure, she could never compare to Jane physically and maybe she wasn't as sweet as Jane but she wasn't that bad. She cringed, feeling like the unkind ugly duckling. A part of her rallied, telling herself not to criticise, to be positive. Besides, today wasn't about her, it was about Jane.

The host stepped back.

This was it, the moment of truth. She glanced at Jane, wanting to see the look on her face when her name was announced.

"Lizzy."

What?

The moment took on an air of unreality. She looked around, amazed to find everyone looking at her, every camera pointed at her. Surely Charles hadn't just said *her* name?

Jane squeezed her hand this time and urged her forward, but when Lizzy looked back there were unshed tears in her eyes.

The walk across the ballroom was the longest of her life. It was like she was headed towards her execution, not to lovely, *lovely*, seriously misguided, Charles. It felt like she was a child playing in her mother's high heels again, wobbling at each step, looking at the floor from a great height. It would be a perfect end to this debacle if she were to fall flat on her face, or her arse.

Finally, she arrived in front of Charles.

He cleared his throat.

"Lizzy, will you accept this bag?"

She knew what she should do. She knew what would be the easiest, the least messy, thing to do.

It was as though a collective breath had been drawn, all were on tenterhooks waiting for her response. Hoping, probably, for something cutting and sarcastic.

But she couldn't do that to Charles.

She glanced back over her shoulder at Jane who was somehow holding it together, though from across the room Lizzy could see the tears quietly making tracks in her cheeks.

She couldn't do this to Jane either.

She opened her mouth, uncertain what she wanted to say. He chose the wrong girl. He shouldn't let other people tell him what to do. His face was so open, expectant, and every eye in the room was on them.

"I–I can't." Her voice came out very small. She tried again. "I'm sorry Charles, I can't."

Why would he do this? To her? To Jane?

Suddenly she couldn't face it anymore. All the cameras, all the faces behind them, all the manipulation. She turned and ran from the room, as best she could in high heels.

**

The ladies' suite was empty – the whole crew had gathered to watch the final ceremony – but she was sure it wouldn't be for long. She struggled with the zip on her dress, twisting and turning. It was so much easier when Jane was there to help, but she managed to step out of the grand affair and be back into her own clothes before anyone arrived. Pressing all the buttons in the elevator may have been childish but had given her the much-needed time.

"You have to go back." It was the guy that Caroline had screamed at earlier in the week. Surely they'd put this guy through enough?

"I don't *have* to do anything," Lizzy replied as she shoved her feet into her shoes. She knelt down and slid her fingers around the edge of her foot to properly guide her foot in. She was really doing it, she was running away. But she'd forgotten about her microphone – now she reached under her top and tore the tape holding it in place. It must have looked like some strange sort of dance, or like she was scratching herself as she traced the line and removed each piece of tape, then finally the power box. "Here," she said finally, placing it in the runner's hands, the cords trailing on the floor. "I'm done."

She left him in the suite and headed for the elevators.

Absurdly she felt like crying. This wasn't how things were meant to end. Charles was supposed to choose Jane and they would live happily ever after. She would smile in the background and hopefully stay friends with Jane once the cameras were off. She sniffed. She would not give them the satisfaction of making her cry.

The boyfriend-handler found her in the lobby as she was making her way across.

"You are under contract—" he started.

"I don't give a shit about your contract," she said. "What happened in there was wrong. I won't be a part of it. Are you *trying* to humiliate Charles?"

He drew himself up to his full height, which wasn't much taller than her. "Of course not, Charles is my friend."

"Oh, so you're the friend who talked him into this. That explains a lot. You care more about your career than your friend. You are a heartless, selfish..." She faltered. *Producer*.

"You want him to choose *Jane*? She's as fake as they come and only in it for the fame. At least I *know* why you're here and you make no qualms about how phoney you think the whole set up is. I don't have to worry about you pretending to be in love with my friend and breaking his heart with your sweet smiles and sly glances. No, Charles chooses you and he's safe."

"You think I'm a *safe* option? How flattering! And what do you mean you know why I'm here?"

"It was made clear early on that you were only here to save your mother's little store from closure. If you're happy to be pimped out to save your mothers business that's fine but—"

"Pimped out? *Pimped out*?!" Lizzy screeched, oblivious to the attention their spat was attracting. "You think my mother is pimping me out? I'm a grown woman and I am not a whore! Sure, I may have agreed to come on this ridiculous excuse for entertainment to give my mother some promotion but that was my choice, *my* choice. And it in no way makes me a whore!" Her chest was heaving with exertion, but she had the bastard on the ropes so she took a deep breath and started again. "You want to talk about whoring someone out? What about what you're doing to your dear friend Charles? You know he's an innocent pawn, you knew he was likely to get his heart broken or trodden all over and you didn't care! This is all about you and your stupid career which you screwed up by fooling around with someone you shouldn't have." She pointed her finger accusingly at him. "This one is on you buddy."

The producer went white. He didn't speak. He glanced around at the crowd they'd attracted – as much of a crowd as a small place like this could boast. Lizzy straightened; she had won this battle. She turned to leave.

"I—"

She turned back. The guy looked like he was still in shock but couldn't find the words to speak. She left him to his silence and exited the hotel with all the dignity she could muster.

Post-Production

JANE: *Lizzy are you ok? You just ran out of there! I'm worried about you*

Lizzy looked at the message, then locked the screen and placed her phone face down on the couch next to her. It was childish but she didn't want to answer Jane. What had been the point in exchanging numbers over pizza? It wasn't like they were friends. They *should* have been rivals. Jane should have been more competitive, instead of so sweet that Lizzy had to defend her. Who was that guy anyway to say that Jane was doing it for the fame? *Had he met Jane?*

The argument ran through her head and raised her blood pressure again, her cheeks heating. *How could he have said those things?* She stared blindly at the sitcom on her TV screen, remembering how pale his face had been at the end. What had he wanted to say before she left?

The manners her mother had drummed into her (see? she was a good mother, not a whoremonger!) battled with her reluctance to talk to anyone. Her training won out in the end. She picked up her phone.

LIZZY: *I'm fine. Thanks for checking on me. I just need some space. Talk soon*

She probably needed to email production to see if she really was in breach of her contract and, if so, what the consequences would be. She wouldn't be able to avoid the villain edit now. But did it matter? It was all fake anyway.

Her mother would be livid. She'd thrown away perfectly good promotion for the store and the chance with a perfectly good guy for what? A woman she'd only known a week who hadn't even kissed him. But it had felt like there was something between Charles and Jane, something too real to be captured by the cameras and lights. And maybe she was a little jealous of that too. Jane was gorgeous, of course she'd get the guy, and Lizzy would be alone again. It had been her mother's wild idea, but there had been a small kernel of hope saying maybe she could have met someone great.

JANE: *Text me if you need to talk*

Jane was too sweet for her own good.

Before she could think herself out of it, Lizzy opened her email on her phone to send a message to production. Surely clearing her email first wasn't avoidance. There were a couple of sales emails she deleted, and something that looked like spam titled "*Please read me*" from someone called William Darcy. She paused, her finger ready to send it to the spam folder, but the preview showed that the email writer at least knew her name. Spam usually couldn't pick her name from her email address. Frowning, she clicked open the message.

Lizzy,

I apologise for my outburst earlier today.

It was unfair of me to intimate that by following your mother's wishes and joining the cast of Bag a Boyfriend *you were in any way cheapening yourself. Your mother made her motivations very clear when we filmed at her shop but that doesn't mean her motivations are the same as yours.*

You implied that I did not have Charles' best interests at heart. You may not be aware that this is not the first time we've attempted to film this show. We were filming for a more mainstream audience but things did not end well and the production was cancelled. Our first "boyfriend" was not someone I knew before filming. He had been vetted, but apparently not well enough. My own sister was one of the contestants and witnessing the manipulation that man put her through was not pleasant. He played the women off against each other, encouraged in-fighting and coerced the women into meeting him off camera. It was a very toxic environment and when one of the women revealed to us the extent of it, we shut production down.

We all signed an NDA so I'm unable to go into further detail. Suffice it to say that my sister was devastated and I reacted as I think any brother would. It cost me my standing with the production company and my means of income.

I still liked the concept and thought it could be successful with a firmer hand and a kinder "boyfriend". I trust Charles implicitly and knew he would be perfect for the role. What I hadn't taken into account is how protective I would feel, as it seems this sort of show attracts a certain type of person. I made it my business to understand each of the contestant's motivations before filming. Jane is a former model, she freely admitted this in her screenings and even provided us with some of her work; that was all the information I needed to know she was trying to reignite her former career.

I could see that Charles, though cautious, was developing genuine feelings for Jane but I couldn't see any evidence that she was interested in anything other than how she appeared on camera. I admit, I steered him towards you as a safer option. Though it appeared to me you were only fulfilling your mother's wishes, you also understood the falseness of the show so would not lead my friend on for continued publicity.

The production will not be pursuing you for breach of contract. There may no longer be a show to save – but I don't blame you for this. It is my own fault and I accept responsibility.

William Darcy

Lizzy stared at her phone, stunned. She had read the email so quickly she barely processed it. She read it again. It appeared the arrogant producer was admitting fault. How must he feel after having two productions fail – and his own sister hurt in the mix? But his assessment of Jane was all wrong. True, Jane did treat everyone with kindness and consideration, and she had freely admitted she hadn't kissed Charles despite her feelings for him. Charlotte had pointed out Charles' feelings for Jane but hadn't mentioned Jane's feelings for him, so maybe they weren't perceptible. It wasn't like Jane was particularly open about her feelings. There was nothing wrong with being a private person, but perhaps it was a disadvantage in these circumstances if the camera didn't see everything.

Why had Jane never mentioned being a model? It made sense – she had the looks for it, if not the personality. She was too good for that shallow world. She taught kindergarten! Though, that wasn't likely to be a lucrative career.

The whole debacle of last night seemed unreal. How much of it had been recorded? Worse - how much of it would appear on the show? Would the show ever air at all? Poor William, to lose two shows.

Poor William? What was wrong with her? He'd treated them terribly and hadn't kept a close enough eye on the first run of the show – it appeared the boyfriend had been accepting, probably suggesting, sexual favours from the contestants to maintain their place. That was all his fault, he admitted it. When it came to his sister she paused; no brother would want their sister in that position, their value as a woman narrowed down to their physical body. She was surprised he hadn't seen it as the pinnacle of how the format treated women. But, he did need to make a living somehow, and they did sign up for it of their own free will. The show wasn't asking them to do anything – the boyfriend was.

Her former self, from university days, would have been disgusted. She'd always been a feminist, indeed she believed anyone with any sense was – no one wanted to return to the dark ages – but during that period she'd been particularly strident. What would she have said to herself?

How did she end up in this situation? Had being involved in this travesty been supporting the patriarchy?

Too many thoughts followed on from a week of too little sleep. Though she had a policy of never drinking alone she decided to break it, just this once, to have a glass of wine and a good sleep. Maybe by the time she got back to work on Monday the whole thing would have blown over.

"Lizzy, how did the show go?"

"I'm contractually forbidden from discussing it," she said for the sixth time that morning. Every person in the office wanted to hear about her week off. She had been obliged to tell Denny why she needed the leave and had sworn him to secrecy, which he obviously had not honoured. The small design firm where she was office manager was a hot-bed of gossip, everyone knew everything about everyone else's lives. She'd been optimistic to suppose this would be any different.

If the show ever aired she was allowed to make some comment on the proceedings but not to shatter the illusion. And if it never aired, well, she'd happily take it to the grave.

Through gritted teeth she smiled at her co-worker, as though this didn't bother her at all, and they went about their day.

She had a ton of emails to catch up on. Lots of requests for stationery, a couple of vendors that hadn't been paid which she flagged to investigate with their accountant. She buried herself in work and managed to skip lunch so she was starving by the time 5:30 rolled around.

In the supermarket, hoping to pick up a heat-and-eat meal, she saw Caroline. Lizzy wondered if they'd always been running into each other before they met but had never realised. It seemed too convenient that Caroline had popped up now. Perhaps it wasn't a coincidence, perhaps Caroline had sought her out. Not wanting to play into any possibly nefarious plans Lizzy turned around and walked down another aisle. Maybe she could get something in a can instead or she could get take out. She wandered aimlessly for a few minutes then made her way back to the fridge section – surely Caroline would be gone now? The coast was clear.

Lizzy gave a sigh of relief and went back to contemplating her dinner. But she froze when she heard from behind her, "Lizzy, is that you?" She had relaxed too soon. Pasting a smile on her face she turned around to greet Caroline.

But it wasn't Caroline.

"Mary?" was all that came out of her mouth. She wasn't sure if this was better or worse than running into Caroline.

"I thought it was you."

Lizzy recovered herself. "I'm surprised you recognised me. You were only there for a day and spent most of it reading." She cringed, realising the words might be taken as harsh, but Mary didn't seem to mind.

"I'm completing my PhD in literature. I technically didn't have time to do the show but reality TV is my guilty pleasure so I couldn't pass up the opportunity."

"Wow, Mary, that's so great." Lizzy wasn't sure if she was talking about the PhD or the dream fulfilment.

"Yeah, in a couple of weeks I'll have my final manuscript to my supervisor for revision then a month or two after that I get to defend my thesis. If all goes well you can address me as Doctor." She said this in a bit of a rush, the last words arcing up as though she was trying to convince them both.

Lizzy smiled at her former competitor. "Charles really wasn't your intellectual equal, was he? I don't even know if he finished uni."

"He didn't. I asked. I find that asking is the best way to discover information. Speaking of – how did the rest of the show go?"

"Mary, you know I'm not allowed to talk about that. I signed an NDA."

"So did I." She smiled, waiting for Lizzy to catch up.

Lizzy frowned, then realisation dawned. "Oh, so you're saying that since we're under the same NDA we're allowed to talk to each other?"

"Technically, yes. I'm not usually much of a gossip but, like I said, reality TV is my thing and this is too good an opportunity to turn down. I mean, that is, if you want to? I don't want to interrupt your...plans?" She eyed the heat-and-eat meal in Lizzy's hands.

"There's a place on the corner where we could get dinner?" Lizzy suggested, putting the package back into the chiller.

Lizzy followed Mary through the checkout and into the street. They didn't bump into Caroline. Once they were seated in the restaurant Lizzy confessed that they'd almost had a run in with the bitchy one.

"Oh, I like the nicknames. Who was I? Or did I not get one because I wasn't there long enough?"

"You were the brainy one, or the smart one. I figured...since you were always reading...and it turns out that I was right, Dr Mary..." she trailed off, realising she didn't know Mary's surname.

A server came to take their order, during which time Lizzy studied Mary and wondered how much it had taken for her to approach someone who was almost a stranger. She hadn't seemed the social type during filming but Mary was in her element now and dominated the conversation.

"So, tell me who won. No, who was the best drama? Ooh, was there a cat fight? I love when they have cat fights. Was it all as orchestrated as the first night?"

"It just got worse. Um, let me see. Technically, I 'won' but I walked out—" Mary gasped "—it should have been Jane. There were no cat fights, though Caroline screamed at the crew at least once a day. And it was every bit as managed as it was the first night. It was a farce."

"You–you walked out? No one has *ever* rejected the bachelor—"

"Boyfriend."

"Whatever. Lizzy, you are a living legend. You've just made reality TV history!" Mary looked at her in awe.

"Yay?" She frowned. "Hold on, *you* rejected him too. I'm not even the first to reject this specific bachelor-boyfriend." She tapped the table to emphasise her words.

Mary look told her she was an idiot. "Sure, sure people walk out early on in the game but not at the final hurdle Lizzy. You were *chosen* and you said no. That's a big deal."

Over the meal Mary sprinkled in anecdotes of various other contestants who had rejected the bachelor, including a Pasifika woman on the first New Zealand incarnation of the franchise who was "far too good for him."

"We don't play the game the same way as they do overseas, more walkouts than internationally."

"I guess I'm just following the trend."

"Were you just not interested in Charles, who was – to be fair – a bit of a wet blanket, or did you object to the obvious structuring of the narrative?"

"Ah...the second one?"

"Fair enough, I could *not* have endured more than I did that one day. Did you know they wanted me to wear glasses? When I told them

I don't need glasses they told me I could just wear frames, like that comedian who got laser surgery and then realised his glasses were integral to his public persona. What if I'd been recognised and then had to wear frames for the rest of my life? With no lenses? What would be the point? And although it may not be obvious on camera, I'm reasonably sure you'd notice if I was sitting across from you. Don't you think you'd notice if I was wearing glasses without lenses in them right now?"

"Ah, yes?" Lizzy reeled from the longest speech she'd ever heard Mary utter.

"And I object to high heels, as a mechanism of the patriarchy to keep women in their place."

"They make my feet hurt." Lizzy offered.

"Exactly."

The dinner was more enjoyable than Lizzy had expected. Mary was unintentionally funny, monologuing about the patriarchy, then enthusiastically dipping back into *The Bachelor* universe, of which they were now apparently members, unable to see the glaring hypocrisy of her beliefs.

"Look at us," she declared waving her arm across the table, "every single one of us blonde. It's like they didn't try. Viewers were not impressed when one of the Bachelors got rid of anyone with any melanin, said he was dating every blonde in the country but this was just ridiculous. Charles had no options. What if he preferred brunettes?"

Lizzy didn't know how to answer.

"This has been a unique bonding opportunity," Mary concluded their interactions. "Would you like to maintain contact?"

They swapped numbers. Lizzy assumed she'd never hear from Mary again.

A week later Lizzy was reviewing the monthly invoices when her desk phone rang. No one ever rang the desk phone, they'd been debating getting rid of them to save costs. It was Denny.

"Oh thank god you're in the office. Everyone else I called was out on assignment."

"You're welcome?" As the office manager it was her job to, well, man, no, woman, no, person....it was her job to be in the office.

"I've forgotten some of the designs for the client this morning. Can you bring them to me? Please? It's a vineyard, I bet if we ask they'd give us free wine or... I could buy you some wine? I know it's not in your job description but I need you."

"You really need a PA." *And possibly a mother.*

"Does that mean you'll do it?"

She agreed.

"You can run my life anytime you like."

She declined and pointed out again that he should get a PA. It was an old argument between them; he was great at the design side of the business but not so much the practical, and she often had to fill in the gaps.

Lizzy consulted Denny's calendar to find where he was, as he had forgotten to tell her, and selected the correct designs from the piles of paper on his desk. One of these days she really needed to bully him into cleaning it. Who knew what might be lurking under there.

The drive out of town was pleasant, passing fields full of vines which may have been part of the property she was visiting; so much of the surrounding area was vineyards it was hard to tell where one ended and another began. Finally, she got to a driveway and passed a little sign on a stick thrust into the soil; Pemberley. If the GPS hadn't warned her she would have missed it. As she drew up to the main house it looked familiar, then it dawned on her. Last time she'd been here it had been covered in crew; it was a shooting location. The setting for one of her dates with Charles.

She drew in next to Denny's car and pulled on the handbrake harder than was necessary. Just as she'd begun to get that whole television debacle out of her head it bounced back into her life. Inevitably she was going to come across places she associated with the show. They had shot all over town after all; best to get used to it now.

Denny was not hovering on the porch waiting for her like she'd hoped, so she couldn't make a quick escape. The house was large with a wraparound porch in a clearing amongst the vines. She mounted the porch steps and walked up to the big front door which was wide open. Should she walk in? Should she knock? Would the owners recognise her if she met them? She couldn't recall if she'd met them last time, it was all such a blur.

She settled on both knocking and walking in, she also called out, "Denny?"

"Tastings are the next driveway along."

Lizzy swung around to face the voice, which came from a beautiful woman with strawberry blonde hair in the doorway, they were about the same height but she looked a few years younger. Where had she come from?

"I'm sorry—" Lizzy began.

"It's fine. It happens all the time." Her smile was apologetic. "We need clearer signage. Actually we're talking with someone about that today." The woman stepped back to usher Lizzy out the door.

"Yes, that's why I'm here," stalled Lizzy, lifting her armload of papers. "The designer asked me to bring these."

"Oh. I'm sorry, I thought—" She blushed and looked down.

Lizzy was surprised how quickly the woman lost her confidence. "It's fine. Sorry for barging in like this, the door was open. Do you–Could you maybe help me? I'm looking for Denny. The designer. His car's out front so I assume he's around here somewhere."

"He'll be meeting with the manager. I'm Gina by the way, I guess I own this place, half of it anyway."

Lizzy adjusted the papers and shook her soft hand; Gina must have someone else do all the vineyard work. How on earth had someone so young come to be in possession of an entire vineyard?

"Oh, I'm Lizzy. I work for Meryton designs. Nice to meet you."

Gina edged past her to lead her into the house.

"I wanted to be a designer at one point," Gina said. "Now I just try to capture the colours of the vines as the seasons change. I don't think the structure of designing for other people would really work for me."

"I'm not a designer. I just manage the office...and sometimes bring designs to meetings." She bit her tongue to avoid adding, "when the designer forgets them".

Gina led her to the back of the house, her movements graceful, to a beautiful room lined with shelves. "This is the library, or was the library – we use it as an office space now."

Denny was waiting alone in the room. He was pleased to see her, thanked her profusely, and offered to have her stay for the meeting but she declined. Gina had disappeared so she headed back to her car. As she was unlocking it she heard someone call her name.

Assuming it was Denny or Gina she walked back around her car. On the steps of the house was the producer of *Bag a Boyfriend*, William Darcy.

"What the hell are you doing here?" burst out of her. Luckily, she was either too far away for him to hear or he pretended not to.

He hurried down the steps to meet her where she stood, frozen, next to the boot of her car. The sun shining down on him created red highlights in his brown hair.

"Lizzy," he said when he reached her. They stood for a moment before he offered his hand for her to shake. She accepted. His hand was warm with just a hint of roughness which made her wonder how it would feel against her bare skin.

"William Darcy, I assume?"

"Right, we've not technically met before, have we?" He winced, remembering. "We only really talked that one time..."

"Yelled is a more accurate description." She mentally kicked herself. "Um, what are you doing here? I didn't expect to see you here. Are they filming more scenery shots or something?"

He'd seemed so intimidating before, perhaps because of his role. Now he just looked, well, uncertain.

William looked down at his feet and kicked a stone. "Actually...this is my house."

"Oh, but I thought..." she trailed off, realising with a twinge of unexpected regret that Gina must be his wife. "Did you–did you want something? From me, I mean?" Shouldn't he be meeting with Denny, rather than talking to her?

"No, I just..." He was looking anywhere but at her. "Gina told me you were here and I knew the name of the firm we were using and it seemed like it had to be you. I remembered where you worked from your application—"

"You remember that from my application?" Something fluttered inside her stomach but she stamped the feeling down; he was married.

"I had to, you know, look at it, to get your details to email you." He finally looked at her and met her gaze. "You did get my email, right?"

A smile broke across her face, unbidden. "That's how I knew your name."

"Right, right." William nodded and swung his arms back and forth. "I didn't hear back from you so I wasn't sure if you..."

Lizzy turned to go. "If that was all?"

"Let me show you around." He seemed surprised by his own outburst, his arm frozen in mid-air, gesturing towards the house.

"I've been here before, remember?" She pressed her lips together; that had come out wrong, accusatory. He dropped his arm. "But I was pretty preoccupied at the time and a personal tour from the owner would be lovely." She forced a smile. "It's a shame the new signage wasn't ready for the show, it would have been great publicity."

"Yeah. I mean – that's not why we did it." He led her around the side of the building. "It was an easy location to manage since we, ah, knew the owners." They shared an awkward smile. "But I'm hoping to splice in a shot of the signage, once it's up, into the finished product."

This brought Lizzy up short. "You mean it's still going ahead, even after I ran out?" she asked incredulously.

William looked around and stopped a few paces ahead of her. "We'd already invested so much money and time..."

She didn't say anything. The words "money and time" echoed in her head. These things were more important to him than the wellbeing of his friend, of Jane, of any of them. Hadn't he proved it over and over again during those long production days?

"There were contracts in place," his tone was pleading, but she ignored it. "Promises had been made. We can't all shirk our responsibilities because of principles."

Her mouth fell open.

William stepped toward her, obviously realising what he'd just said. "I'm sorry, Lizzy, I didn't mean—"

"No, I'm pretty sure you did," she said, impressed with herself for managing to say anything, she was trembling so hard. She turned and raced back to her car, William on her heels.

"Lizzy, please!" But she refused to listen to a word he said, leaping into her car, jamming the key in the ignition and reversing. William leapt out of the way. The tyres tore up the gravel as she backed away then sped down the driveway, pulling on her seatbelt; past the vines, past the empty space at the gate, and away from William Darcy – hopefully to never see him again.

"You must have made an impression last week," Denny said, leaning against her desk.

"Huh?" Lizzy looked up from the spreadsheet where she'd been trying to track one of the junior designers' hours, it looked like they weren't billing sufficient hours to meet the requirements of their contract.

"They invited us to an event next month and specifically mentioned you."

"Who did what now?" Lizzy frowned. She wanted to tell Denny to buzz off so she could focus, but she'd been snippy enough lately that people had commented on it. She was trying to rein herself in. She sighed in frustration and physically turned herself away from her screen to focus on Denny.

"The vineyard. They're having a party to unveil the new signage. Of course we're invited, but they specifically asked if *you* could attend. What did you say to them?"

"I—" She tried to remember exactly what she'd said. Had she called William a pompous arse or just thought it? She vividly recalled narrowly avoiding him with her car and had been surprised to arrive back in town in one piece, fuelled by rage with no recollection of the drive. "Gina and I talked about art," she said finally, grasping at a straw. "She paints the vines, likes the colours. I'm not sure why she didn't do the sign herself."

"Well, let's be glad she didn't as it's work for us. We've got those two big signs, at the main entrance and the private entrance. Plus updating all the signage around the property to match the new branding and a little side work on their promotional materials too. Potential future work for events there, they said they'd recommend us to their clients. It'll be a good pay day."

"So, when is this thing? Do I have to go?" She sounded uncomfortably like a whiny teenager. She tried to counteract this with a smile. "I mean, do you want me to go?"

"They could throw a lot of work our way, Lizzy," Denny was already turning away but threw back over his shoulder, "I'll email you the details."

Great. Another obligation. One which meant she'd have to see William Darcy again. He owned the place, he would be there. Perhaps she could manage to spend the night avoiding him. It was just like him to pull strings, force her into seeing him when he had to know she'd rather hit him with her car.

Jane would have told her off for that thought. She still hadn't responded to Jane's text from several weeks ago. It wasn't fair to avoid her.

LIZZY: I suck. Obviously. Sorry for not replying sooner. I'm fine. Life just got in the way

JANE: You don't suck Lizzy. Are you sure you're ok? Would you like to catch up in person?

She wasn't sure so she avoided both questions.

LIZZY: I'm back at work which is good. How is your work?

JANE: The kids were so excited to have me back and I missed them. They change so much in such a short space of time!

She could almost feel Jane smiling through the phone. Her text conversation with Jane carried her through afternoon; she left the office with a smile on her face.

**

Lizzy had pushed the vineyard party to the back of her mind, hoping it might somehow disappear. She'd been avoiding Jane's invitation to meet, sure she'd blurt everything out and Jane would be disappointed in her behaviour.

She spent the week of the event dealing with enquiries from an entitled high school student whose parents thought they could buy good grades. They were trying to palm an assignment off on the designers.

Just read it through and make any changes, their email had read.

Lizzy had to explain, as politely as she could, that it wasn't a service they offered. Formatting, diagrams and other images, yes, but the student needed to hire an editor. Lizzy had, in the past, done a once-over of the material they received from clients but she wasn't about to do it for someone else's assignment.

What kid had the sort of money to hire professionals to pretty up their work? But it gave her an idea.

"Do you think we need to bring an editor on board? Or a writer? Maybe someone we can contract in when we need them?" Lizzy asked in the team meeting. "Or maybe we build another offering and hire someone full time? I don't mind assessing clients' copy but I'm not sure I know what I'm doing."

The designers glanced at each other, seemingly unwilling to comment on something that was out of their area of expertise too.

"It's a good idea," Forster, the accountant, began. "Another string to our fiddle. Presumably we'd be on-charging their time to client billing so we could certainly afford to hire someone. Perhaps we could start them on a contract basis then move to something more full time if the workload builds up. Denny, what do you think?"

Everyone turned to look at Denny, seated half way down the table; he liked to be in the middle of his staff rather than reigning over them from one end. "Write me a proposal. Lizzy, Forster, work together on the numbers, look back at some of our previous clients and see where we could have added value. Make some calls, see if there's an appetite for it. Now, we have the unveiling at the Pemberley vineyards this evening. Show of hands, who's coming?"

Lizzy groaned and raised her hand, along with about half the others seated around the table. She'd planned to "forget" if Denny hadn't brought it up.

"Great, great. I'm sure it'll be a good night. Now, there will be free wine but please don't overdo it, we need to maintain some professionalism. Remember, these are our clients. Lizzy – " her head snapped up " – can you order transport to take us from the office?"

She nodded and Denny closed the meeting.

Nervous and dressed to the nines Lizzy drove back to work to catch the transport to the vineyard; she planned on being able to drive herself home but if she couldn't it would be easier if her car were at work than at the vineyard. Her makeup wasn't as perfect as Maria would have made it – nor anywhere near as heavy – but she was proud of her efforts.

Forster was the first one there, waiting. He complimented her dress; it was nothing compared to the monstrosities she'd been wearing on camera, but he couldn't know that. He quickly turned the conversation to her proposal that they hire an editor.

"With service sites popping up all over we won't be able to be competitive financially. We'll have to use the integrated service as a selling point. But there is still a possibility that we'll get push back from clients who are accustomed to cheap overseas labour."

"Surely they aren't our sort of clients though? If you want a cheap service why bother engaging us at all? There are sites which cater to design too."

Forster nodded. "Occasionally we still get custom from people who've tried to do it themselves and realised their mistake. I can only hope that what happened with design will predict editing too. We'll run the numbers on Monday," he finished up, as other colleagues started to approach.

They piled into the van to wait for Denny, Lizzy shifting her skirt and the men adjusting their ties. There was a whiff of beer – some of the younger designers had been pre-loading.

"Denny says he'll meet us there," one of the designers said, their face illuminated by their phone screen.

"That's us," Lizzy said to the driver, and pulled the door closed.

The drive was different in the dark; they were soon out of street lights, driving into emptiness. Lizzy wondered if they had thought to light the signage – it could be difficult to find the place in the dark. *Perhaps we'll end up driving around for hours and miss the event entirely.*

She was disappointed to see the prominent sign looming ahead. "Pemberley". They'd done a good job *and* the sign was illuminated.

No escaping now, no walking back to town in these heels. Why should she avoid William though? She hadn't done anything to be ashamed of. If anything, *he'd* been the one pimping out his friend and his property for the show.

With this cheery thought she thanked the driver and reminded him to return in two hours. Surely she could survive two hours? She trailed behind her colleagues, hoping to hide. Unfortunately there was some sort of receiving line, so each person marched past the hosts to introduce themselves.

"Gina, hi. Nice to see you." She shook the woman's hand. "William." She nodded at him politely and stepped away before he could say anything.

Then she was free to roam the exquisite room, make small talk and sip wine. A string trio was playing in the far corner, the sound carrying throughout the space.

Bill Lucas found her. He didn't seem quite comfortable holding the stem of a wine glass – at a guess she'd say he was more of a whiskey man but at a vineyard he had to act the Roman.

"Capital property," he started. "I've been trying to get them to sell for some time. Old family, you know."

Lizzy forced a smile. "How nice to see you again."

"Any of the other contestants here?" Bill looked over her shoulder, then made a show of looking around the room.

"Not that I know of. I'm here because I work for the design firm. Not because of the production."

"Ah." He seemed disappointed. "Charles is around here somewhere."

Lizzy felt the blood drain from her face. "R–really? I, um, didn't know that I–I don't think I'm allowed to see him – under contract, you understand. Maybe I should go?"

She turned to leave but Bill called her back.

"Nonsense, nonsense." He waved her mention of the contract away. "I'm sure it's all above board. Ho-ho, I suppose you haven't seen him since your exit, have you? Now I know why you want to run away." He gave a knowing smile and sipped from his glass, pulling a face.

She raised her eyebrows at his expression and he had the decency to look abashed. "I don't normally drink wine, you see." He nodded at her glass. "Do you like it? I can't tell if it's any good."

Lizzy looked at the glass in her hand. She couldn't recall if she'd drunk any of it yet. She'd been too nervous on her date with Charles to really appreciate the wine. She took a cautious sip.

Of course William Darcy would make good wine. No wine would dare disobey him.

"It's good," she nodded. Probably the best local wine she'd tasted. All the wine on dates throughout production was probably from this vineyard, not that she recalled the taste – everything was sponsored and clearly William would do anything for publicity.

"You were saying there wasn't anyone else here!" exclaimed Bill. "But there she is."

Lizzy swung around expecting to see Jane, but bearing down on them was Caroline; the second to last person Lizzy wanted to see.

"Bill," Caroline trilled. "How delightful to see you." She pressed her cheek to his and kissed the air; Lizzy had never seen the move in real life before and was impressed despite herself. "Who are you—" She turned and her whole demeanour changed. "Oh. Lizzy, was it?" Caroline was so accomplished at looking down her nose that Lizzy imagined she'd be able to do it even if she wasn't taller than whoever she was condescending to.

"Caroline, I didn't expect to see you here." Lizzy tried to inject some enthusiasm into her voice.

"Oh, I'm at all the big events around town." Caroline showed her teeth and slid an arm through Bill's. "Aren't I, Bill?"

Bill blushed and stuttered. Lizzy stared – she had never seen him so unsure of himself. An awkward silence reigned while Caroline patted the front of Bill's suit, removing imaginary lint, quite clearly marking her territory. Either she didn't know Charles was here or she had decided Bill was a bigger catch. The media would love that! "*Former Contestant Dating Host.*"

Caroline finally looked at Lizzy again and a made a noise which Lizzy interpreted as "Oh, you're still here?"

"I work for the design firm who did the recent updates," Lizzy offered.

"Oh that's right. You make the coffee."

Lizzy smirked. "I order it too. I don't think we talked about what sort of work you do, Caroline." She wasn't sure they'd ever had a proper conversation. Caroline had occasionally talked, but more at her than *to* her.

"I work in publicity," she said shortly.

"That must be really interesting. What does that involve?"

Bill jumped, Lizzy could see the tight grip Caroline had him in. What was that about? "Ah-ah, let's not talk about work at a party," he said. "Let's talk about... how great this wine is!" He drained his glass then with a pained expression continued, "isn't it great?"

"I hear you won," Caroline said, her tone challenging.

"I'm sorry, won what exactly?" Lizzy asked innocently.

Caroline rolled her eyes. "*Bag a Boyfriend.* Charles picked you. For some reason."

Lizzy gave the brightest false smile she could. "I'm sorry, I'm under contract and therefore unable to discuss the outcome of the show. You can find out what happened when it airs, like everyone else."

"Well..." Bill began.

"It's been lovely seeing you both, but I must go." She gave a cheery wave but let the smile slip from her face as soon as her back was turned. Where the hell was Denny? Hopefully he'd let her go home, she had drunk a glass of wine – she looked at her glass – well, half a glass, and she'd spoken to two people. Surely that was enough?

A scan of the room revealed Denny talking to a woman over in the far corner. Was it worth risking his wrath and leaving, or should she risk battling her way across the room to ask his leave? She had decided on the latter approach when who should she spot but William Darcy, a sight which necessitated a change in plans. To avoid him she snuck outside into the cool night air. She took a deep breath and let her shoulders drop.

"Are you a smoker, or an introvert like me?" came a voice, startling her. "Smokers are congregating around the back."

Lizzy swung around and Gina appeared from the shadows. "I hate these sorts of things," Gina confessed. "Too many people in one room."

"I can go if I'm invading your quiet time?"

Gina smiled. "I can handle a one-on-one." Then she winced at the reality TV show terminology. "I mean, you're Lizzy, right? My brother talks about you all the time."

"He does? I don't think I know your brother."

"He says that..." she swallowed and looked at the ground, watching the toe of her shoe make marks in the dirt. "He says that *you* should have been on the first season, you would have put George in his place." She glanced up, then down again.

Lizzy stepped closer. "I'm sorry... I..." Then it fell into place – Gina wasn't William's wife, she was his sister! The sister who had been abused by the boyfriend on the first incarnation of *Bag a Boyfriend*. "Your...brother is pretty good at putting people in their place himself. Did he tell you we had a screaming match in the hotel lobby? It was not pretty. I'm not sure either of us came out the winner. Anyway, all I really did was walk away."

"But that takes so much courage!" Gina stepped back into the shadows, surprised at her own outburst. "I mean, if it had been me, I wouldn't have been able to do that. I would have probably dated the guy till he dumped me for someone better." She gave a bitter laugh. "And he wouldn't have the decency to tell me himself, I'd find out through the papers."

Lizzy looked down at the glass she was still holding. She really should have left it inside so she could leave without anyone noticing. She took another sip while she contemplated how to answer Gina. *She's his sister, not his wife...*

"It must be nice to have a brother. I don't have any siblings; only child, which I guess makes me independent. My mother was–is...interesting. She has all these ideas about me being a strong woman but she also wants me to follow traditional gender roles. Get married, have kids. She's the reason I was even on the show. She sent in my application without telling me." For the first time it occurred to her that in a perverse way her mother was trying to provide for her, even though her own marriage hadn't lasted.

Gina stepped forward again. "Our parents are dead—"

"Oh God! I'm so sorry, I—"

"No, no, it's ok. You didn't know. How could you know? This place was their dream. Neither William or I know a thing about wine, I don't even like drinking it. But we keep it going in their memory. It's beautiful whether you're a fan of wine or not. This sort of thing though," she tilted her head to indicate the building behind them with the party going on, "isn't really my scene. But I have to show my face."

"My boss made me come," Lizzy confessed and they both laughed. "Do you think you can brave it again? Maybe if we make an appearance together...."

Gina took the glass from Lizzy's hand. "How about I drop this inside and we head up to the house for a cup of tea instead?"

**

"These are gorgeous." Lizzy was seated on a squashy couch, her legs tucked up under her, hated heels abandoned on the floor, looking at Gina's sketch book. "Of course, I know nothing about art. But I like them."

She turned a page and there was William Darcy. Several studies of him in different attitudes. She lingered on an image of him, half profile as though he was turning towards the viewer. He looked calmer than she was used to him looking, a half-smile on his face. Perhaps that was because the only times she'd talked to him they'd argued.

Gina handed her a mug of tea and sat at the other end of the sofa, cradling her own mug. "That's kind of you. I'm just an amateur but I do love it. William's really supportive, always allowing me to draw him. Weirdly, he doesn't like looking at pictures of himself though."

"The guys at work – it's an entirely different discipline – the computer makes everything 3D. But this takes real skill, natural talent. I'm not sure it's something you can learn."

"Everything can be learnt with the right teacher."

Gina started talking about art she'd seen on a trip to Italy, but mention of the word "teacher" made Lizzy think of Jane. They'd had a few text conversations; it sounded like Jane was happy, but they studiously avoided any mention of Charles. At least, Lizzy did; she wasn't sure if Jane was avoiding the topic too or whether it never occurred to her. Could someone fall in love over a week with cameras tracking their every interaction? Then she remembered Bill saying that Charles was at the party, maybe she should...not confront him exactly...just...talk to him. Maybe he deserved an apology. Maybe.

"How's your social battery?" Lizzy asked Gina.

She looked at the ceiling and groaned in response. "You want me to go back, don't you?"

"You don't have to. But there's someone there that I should probably talk to." Gina pulled a 'tell me more' face. "Ok, fine. It's Charles."

Gina shook her head. "Why do you want to talk to Charles? How do you even know... Oh, of course. He was your 'boyfriend', wasn't he?" She made air quotes around the word. "Are you still into him?"

"No. Not exactly. He's a nice guy. He's just...not for me. Maybe, just maybe, it was rude of me to walk out on him? I may have ulterior motives. One of the other women on the show – I think she really, I mean *really*, liked him. She hasn't mentioned him once since we left the show. Doesn't that say something?"

Gina shifted in her seat. "I didn't stay in contact with the women from the show. They were...*weren't*...It wasn't a good experience." Her fingers plucked at the fabric of the couch.

"Do you want to talk about it?"

"NDA says I can't."

"Right. Right." She didn't want to leave Gina when she was upset but she didn't know what to say or do. She closed the sketch book and placed it on the table. She decided it would be easiest to share her own *Bag a Boyfriend* experience. "Charles was different, you know? He seemed as reluctant to be there as I was. He didn't seem the sort to...he was different. I don't think I'd ever met any of the women before but I can't avoid them now, they're everywhere I go. One of them is here tonight. I also narrowly avoided running into her at the supermarket a couple of weeks ago." She realised she'd yet to text Mary to ask about the progress of her PhD.

"I used to love those shows, before I was part of one." Gina looked into her mug. "I've finished my tea. I don't suppose I have an excuse anymore."

"Don't feel you have to go back just because I want to."

But Gina insisted on accompanying her back to the party. "William won't tell us off if we're together," was said with a smile which seemed to hint at a hidden meaning. She shook off her dark thoughts and even managed to laugh when Lizzy offered to introduce her to Charles, who she'd known for years.

"There he is," Gina said as they entered the building. But it wasn't Charles coming towards them, it was William.

Lizzy interrupted his compliments on her appearance with, "We snuck out. But it was my fault. We had tea and talked about art."

William smiled warmly and suddenly Lizzy was a gauche girl, dressed in her mother's clothes, talking to a handsome man in a fine suit. Gina squeezed her arm as William spoke.

"I want you two to get to know each other. I'm glad you came. I wasn't sure you were going to after our last encounter."

"Ha. Well. Perhaps we're best not to examine that, ah...encounter." She pulled her shoulders back; her mother would not be impressed with her posture.

There was nothing to say. They stood in awkward silence for a moment then William started talking about what a great job her colleagues had done on the designs. She agreed and mentioned a couple of team members in particular, pointing them out in the crowd. Gina chimed in with a wish that she could do that sort of work too, which led to a discussion of digital art versus pen and paper.

Some time later Lizzy noticed Charles coming their way, and wondered whether she should back out the door to avoid him. Ensconced on the couch with Gina he seemed like a different prospect than standing in a room full of people with nowhere to hide. But she'd done nothing wrong. If she could manage awkward arduous conversation with the Darcy siblings – however sweet Gina was, she wasn't a great conversationalist – then she could face her former "boyfriend."

"Lizzy," he said as he reached them. "I didn't expect to see you here." He smiled at Gina and William who allowed him entry into their little circle.

"My company did the designs."

"Your company?"

"Oh, I mean, I just work for them."

"And does a great job by all accounts," Darcy said. "Even ran all the way out here to deliver designs for a meeting. Keeps the whole office ticking over, I'm told."

Lizzy nodded and looked at her feet, unsure what to say.

"It's been–it's been some time since I saw you," Charles said. When she nodded he continued, "Not since, well, you know. It was a good night, a good week. I had a good time." Lizzy looked up at this and saw him glancing at William as though checking he wasn't about to be reprimanded. "It's a shame though, isn't it, that we didn't stay in contact? Have you been in contact with any of the other...er...women?"

Lizzy smiled. He was asking about Jane, right? "Well...Caroline is around here somewhere," she said, pretending to look for her.

Charles looked slightly terrified. "I have seen her, yes. But any of the *other* women, at all?"

"I had dinner with Mary. Did you know she's about to become a doctor? Not an MD, a PhD."

He looked crestfallen. "No, I didn't. Ah, good for her."

She took pity on him; it wasn't fair to torture him when William had been the one to make him reject Jane. "I've had several conversations with Jane. We haven't met up yet though. She's glad to be back at work." She turned to Gina as she added, "She's a kindergarten teacher you know. The sweetest person you'll ever meet." She glanced up at William, expecting a frown but he seemed perfectly happy with the conversation.

"Is she–is she seeing anyone?" Charles asked, his voice rising in pitch, his eyes darting towards William.

"Not as far as I know." She almost offered him Jane's number, reaching towards her bag before she remembered it wasn't her place. If he wanted it, he could ask. He *should* ask, and she shouldn't be giving out Jane's number willy-nilly without her permission.

Silence reigned again, then Gina spoke. "I'm glad you made friends in your season, Lizzy. You seem like the sort of person who makes friends easily. I'm not great at that myself."

William opened his mouth but Lizzy cut over him. "You're a little shy, that's all. Look how easily you talked to me."

"Will's my best friend," Charles added. "He adopted me. I'm not great at making friends either. You can't compare yourself to your brother, you know. We introverts have to stick together." He nudged Gina's arm.

"Should we go?" William asked Lizzy in an aside. "Leave them to their introverts club?"

"I did *not* have you pegged as an extrovert," she replied with a laugh. "Maybe an extroverted introvert. You appear extroverted because you're surrounded by fellow introverts."

Charles laughed. "Sounds like she knows you."

"Are you a studier of character?" William asked. "What else can you tell me about me?"

Gina laughed this time. "Now you just sound vain. 'Tell me about me.'"

William seemed affronted so Lizzy refrained from laughing at the gibe from his sister.

"You like things to go your way," she said slowly. "That's not a fault though; who doesn't? You look out for those closest to you, but sometimes it may lead you to...not consider how that may impact others. You're very organised, succinct, concise."

Caroline materialised next to Lizzy just as William was leaning forward to say something. "Lizzy, come for a walk with me and meet some people. Oh, hello Charles." She nodded at him briskly and tugged Lizzy's arm. Perhaps she hadn't discarded Charles and wanted to ensure Lizzy didn't snare him. Capitulating to Caroline seemed the easier thing to do, especially in heels. She gave a sad wave to the little group as she left.

Lizzy lay in bed contemplating the night before. Alone, thank you. A slight dull headache reminded her she didn't usually drink that much wine and she was reasonably sure if she peeked in her bathroom mirror there would be remnants of eye makeup too. She'd had a good time though. With a smile she recalled giggling with Gina as they navigated the rows via phone light to escape the party for the quiet of the house, holding skirts out of the way from clutching vines. Gina had led the way there; she had led the way back. Perhaps they should have holed up in the house the whole night. But there had been that short conversation with Charles, proving he did still care for Jane. And there was William too...

She stretched and considered getting up. There was no real reason to; she had no appointments today, no pressing projects, she'd caught up on the TV she missed during production and didn't have the attention span today to read a book. No, the one thing she'd been putting off was seeing Jane.

With a groan Lizzy rolled over and reached for her phone. Better to do it now than keep procrastinating. At this rate she'd be lucky if Jane still considered her a friend at all.

She checked the time...perfect. Just enough time to get up and dress.

LIZZY: *Brunch?*

It was as if Jane had been sitting by her phone waiting for the text as her reply was instantaneous, before Lizzy even turned off the screen.

JANE: *I would love to see you! What time suits you?*

When Lizzy spotted Jane hovering near the café entrance she wished she'd had several hours more sleep, was wearing a full face of make-up and dressed in slightly less rumpled clothes. After so long apart she'd forgotten how stunning Jane was, it was like a kick to her stomach. How could she even speak to this beautiful creature? A smile broke over Jane's face and Lizzy remembered the sweet person on the inside.

Jane's hug was full bodied, not just an arm around the shoulder, Lizzy leaned in unable to remember the last time she'd really been hugged. Jane tidied Lizzy's hair so she laughed and swatted the hand away.

"You don't need to mother me. I'm fine. I promise. Let's get some food."

Jane apologised as they walked over to an empty table, explaining that she did it for the kids. She then stumbled over her words, apologising some more, worried she had just called Lizzy a child. Lizzy laughed it off and asked whether it was difficult to hug kids in the current environment, whether it was allowed.

"We have a poster by the front door with little symbols so they can choose how they want to be greeted. Some kids want a high five or a fist bump instead of a hug. It's very important to instil an understanding of consent and choice to them at a young age. They're less likely to be taken advantage of. It's also a good indicator of how they may be feeling that day; sometimes kids who don't normally want hugs ask for them and you know something's happened at home so you keep a closer eye on them. It works the other way too, some kids just want quiet time and will draw into themselves, you learn to read that and respect it."

"I think I've seen something like that on the internet." Lizzy picked up the menu from the table and flipped it over.

"It's actually where I got the idea. I did some research, got approval and implemented it. The kids love it and the parents seem to appreciate it too. It adds a little structure to the start of each session and settles the kids in."

"Life would certainly be easier if we had those for everyday interactions. Why do women always get hugged? I'm not much of a hugger. Oh, no—" she said as Jane started to protest, "—not you. I just mean in general. Not much of a fan of handshaking either but I could do a high five or a fist bump. Not sure how that would go down in the office...What am I saying? The guys would love it!"

After they ordered and Jane had rearranged the condiments on the table, Lizzy was wondering how to bring up Charles when Jane said, "Have you heard anything about...you know?" She fiddled with the salt shaker, turning it around and around. "Do you know they put rice in the bottom of these to collect the moisture so the salt doesn't clump? I just wondered because I haven't heard anything. It was so weird after you left. There was silence, like everyone was in shock, then everyone started yelling. That wasn't pleasant. I was worried they were going to yell at you." Jane finally looked up and there was real concern on her face. "Then I didn't hear from you. And you were so short in your texts I thought maybe you didn't want to stay in touch. But if you don't that's ok, it's your choice." She dropped the salt shaker and raised her hands. "I'm not going to force you to see me or anything."

Lizzy smiled. "Sweetheart, it's ok. I'm ok. I just needed some time. It was...overwhelming. Of course I want to stay friends with you." She reached out and touched Jane's hand where it lay on the table. "You saved me, you know? If it hadn't been for you, I don't know if I would have had the strength to walk out of there like I did." Something about that sounded overly dramatic, but it was true.

Jane shook her head. "That was all you. I don't know how you did it. With all that pressure, all those lights, all those cameras and people just staring at you, judging your every move. Did I tell you I used to do some modelling? It was terrible. The money was good but the humiliation wasn't worth it. I didn't have the best relationship with my body, but we're on good terms now. I wouldn't give that up for anything. I think working on the show reminded me of that time. *You* saved *me.*"

"I guess it's a mutual appreciation society. No – mutual salvation society."

Their drinks arrived, causing a break in the conversation as Lizzy stirred sugar into hers.

"There was yelling," she admitted, "mostly from me. I'm not comfortable being yelled at, do anything I can to avoid it, but I was so worked up I didn't even notice." She smiled at the memory of William being all riled up, they knew how to press each other's buttons.

"I saw Charles recently," she said and took a sip of coffee, hoping Jane wouldn't ask why she was smiling. "Caroline too. And William, but of course you don't know him."

"Oh?" Jane said casually, but she stiffened and her eyes darted about the room, looking for a distraction. "How–how was he?" She raised her cup to her mouth then put it down again.

"I think he's good. We didn't get much of a chance to talk. He, uh, asked how everyone was but I really think he was asking about you."

"*Really?* I mean," Jane cleared her throat, "that's–that's nice. How was he? Oh right, you said that already. Good. Good." She picked up her mug again and put it down directly. "Where do you suppose the food is? Have we been waiting long?" She looked towards the kitchen, straining her neck.

Lizzy called her attention back to the table. "Can I ask you something? And be honest."

Jane nodded but looked a little scared.

"So, you have feelings for Charles, right?"

"I'm sorry, what was the question?" Jane tucked hair behind her ear.

Lizzy laughed. "I'll take that as a yes. I thought you did, but I couldn't be sure it wasn't just ...situational."

"Honestly, neither could I." Jane sighed and pushed her coffee cup away. "But I still think about him. Something happens and I want to tell him about it, but he's not there, and this is ridiculous – I only spent a week with the guy! A couple of hours really." She took a deep breath then said, "Why do I miss him so much?"

Her voice was loud. The waitress stepped back and almost dropped their food. Jane apologised, and the waitress left.

"I'm a walking cliché," she said more quietly this time. She handed Lizzy cutlery from the container on the table, then took her own but held it in a strangle-hold.

Promising beginnings didn't always go somewhere, but if Jane and Charles had the chance perhaps they could. Was there any likelihood of them ever seeing each other again? She had Gina's number, maybe she could arrange something, whether on purpose or by "accident."

**

"Fancy running into you here." It was William Darcy. The junior designer on reception duty had popped out so Lizzy was holding down the fort.

She rose from behind the front desk, she didn't want him to think she was a receptionist. In his presence she craved equilibrium; she couldn't cope looking up at him. "I do work here, you know." It came out more challenging than intended – it was meant as a joke between friends. Were they friends?

"Right, right. I just came to pay my invoice." He held up a sheet of paper, placed it on the counter.

"Have you heard of internet banking?" She put a smile behind this one.

"Well I—"

Lizzy scanned the desk for an eftpos machine. "I don't think we take payments."

"Right, right." He contemplated his invoice before lowering his voice. "I wanted an excuse to see you."

"That's..." Weird. Exciting. *Exciting?* "Honest."

He looked into her face. "My sister really liked you."

"I liked her." She pressed her lips together, desperate for him to speak. "Was that...all? Our bank details are on the bottom of the invoice."

"Can we go out sometime? I'd like to take you out. Can I take you out?"

She heard herself say, "Is that allowed? I mean, we worked on the show together, my company worked for your vineyard. I just...don't know..." *if I want to*. She'd never considered dating him.

After all, what did she really know about him? Charles said he was a good friend, Gina said he was a good brother – though perhaps a little over protective. He looked crushed, like it had taken a lot for him to come here.

"Right, right," he said again. He pursed his lips, tapped the counter with the invoice which fluttered uselessly. "I'll pay this online."

He turned; she realised if he left she would never see him again. Work had finished, the show had finished. No reason remained for them to meet. Sure, Gina had her number but that didn't mean she'd see *him*. Disappointment hit her stomach like an icy peppermint.

"Would you like my number?" she asked abruptly.

He spun around, a look of disbelief on his face. He opened his mouth but no sound came out.

Lizzy grabbed a paper from the cube – bluey green she noted wildly, as though that were important – and scribbled her number. She then scribbled it out, screwed up the paper and threw it down. Her second attempt was better. She held out her offering. For a split second she thought he wasn't going to accept, then a smile crept across his face. He reached for the paper.

Lizzy almost fell back into her chair after he'd left, not believing what she'd just done but proud of herself. But what would he think if he knew she was plotting to get Charles and Jane in the same room again? Well, they'd have to burn that situation if they came to it.

LIZZY: *I saw your brother today*

It wasn't the most original opener but it would probably get a reaction from Gina. She put her phone back on the battered coffee table her ex-boyfriend had barely managed to put together. Perhaps it was time for an upgrade.

The next boyfriend had better be an upgrade too; he'd said she was too weird. Made too many jokes. Needed to be more serious. Take things more seriously. Take him more seriously. Take their relationship more seriously. She was serious when she ended things. He hadn't liked that.

Dating was something she'd avoided since then, with the reluctant exception of *Bag a Boyfriend*. Though like all her recent forays into dating, that had been her mother's choice. She bit her lip and thought about William, wondering whether she would hear from him or if he'd leave her on the cutting room floor. He had the ball, he just had to hit it to her side of the situationship.

The tune from her phone gave her a jolt, was he calling? Who called these days? But it was her mother's picture on the screen.

"Hi Mum."

"Hello darling. I haven't heard from you in *days*. What if something happened?"

"To you or to me?" She shifted and paused the television; her mother's rants were often lengthy.

"To either of us! I could have a fall or get mugged or—"

"Mum, you are not going to get mugged, we live in New Zealand."

"How do you know? Anything could happen these days. I swear..."

Tuning her mother out, Lizzy examined her nails and considered a manicure. A professional one would last longer but on the other hand she could put her mother on speaker and kill two birds with one phone call. She made consoling noises and got her meagre selection of nail polish from the fridge. She tuned back in to realise her mother was talking about some guy.

"Wait. What? Who?"

The sigh that came down the phone line was almost equal to the size of her mother's disappointment.

"That nice boy from the TV show—" Lizzy paused, one fingernail half base-coated. *Charles?* "This makes it the *third* time he came in. First he came in to discuss how and when they were going to film, then he came in the day they were actually filming, quite terse he was then. But this time Lizzy, he was so polite! Told me he couldn't stop thinking about my fudge and had to come back for more..."

Lizzy dipped the brush back into the polish and continued on her nails.

"Now, I know you can't tell me what happened on the show till it screens—"

"You are completely right, I signed an NDA."

"But I thought—"

"Hold up." Suspicion, paired with knowledge of her mother, sparked a thought. "Didn't you have to sign an NDA too? They were filming in your store. You can't tell anyone what happened either."

"Well, I just happened to mention to..."

"Mum!" She hastily put the brush back in the polish to avoid flinging polish all over the couch as she gestured. "Do you realise how much trouble you could get into for this? NDA's are a big deal." Talking to other cast members and production crew was probably fine though, she hoped. So long as her mother never found out about her double standard.

"This is a small town, dear. Everyone knows everyone's business."

"I am not telling you mine so you can spread it all over town and *I* get in trouble for breaking my NDA. You can find out on screen with everyone else."

"Does that mean you don't want to see this boy again? He's very nice, once you get past his work persona. If I were a few years younger I might just—"

"Please do not finish that sentence. I beg you."

Her mother harrumphed and made a snide comment implying Lizzy hadn't won, or she'd be in a better mood with all the sex was having. Lizzy distracted her by asking about business. The call lasted through two layers of colour, several stories about people her mother knew and Lizzy finished off the top layer worrying about how much of her mother's ridiculousness might have been caught on camera.

Gina texted back while her nails were still drying.

GINA: *Did he behave himself or did you have to give him a smack down again?*

LIZZY: *When is your brother not the perfect gentleman?*

GINA: *He always thought he was till he met you*

Lizzy tapped her phone against her knee, unsure how to respond to that.

GINA: *OMG you gave him your number??*

GINA: *I mean, he's not here. I'm not asking him about you*

Lizzy laughed, picturing William with his hands on his hips, demanding his sister stop relaying his every word via text. Her phone was silent so she unpaused the TV, just in time for the phone to buzz again. It wasn't Gina.

WILLIAM: *Hi, this is William Darcy. Thank you for your help today*

What could she say to that – just doing my job, you're welcome? She paused the TV again and pondered an appropriate response.

WILLIAM: *My sister has just informed me that was a "lame opener". I apologise*

She couldn't help it; she laughed. She put her feet up on the ex-boyfriend coffee table and crossed her ankles. This should be good.

LIZZY: *Would you like to try again? I can pretend I never saw that message*

He didn't answer for a couple of minutes and she worried she'd said the wrong thing. Perhaps she should have included an emoji. She had finally unpaused the television again when his response came through.

WILLIAM: *Hi, it's William. Can I take you to dinner tomorrow night?*

LIZZY: *A flirtatious yes*

WILLIAM: *Sorry, I'm not very good at flirting*

LIZZY: *I'm sure we can work on that* 😊

GINA: *OMG you're going out!!!*

All day at work Lizzy kept wondering where William would take her for dinner, what they would talk about, would it be awkward, what should she wear, did she really like him, was it disloyal to Jane to like him? Questions kept popping into her head. Somehow she finished the proposal to hire an editor and sent it to the accountant.

Ordinarily men didn't learn where she lived for several dates. Sure, it was nice to be picked up at the beginning of the evening, then driven home, but she didn't want to run the risk of the guy trying anything, or him knowing where she lived if he ended up being creepy. But when William asked if he could pick her up she gave him her address without a second thought. It wasn't until she was driving home that she realised. Too late now.

If he'd wanted to he could have discovered a lot of highly personal information, including her sexual activity, if he were to glance in her production file. It was clear he had at least some knowledge from there. It felt a bit Big Brother and it probably should have bothered her more. Where had her principles gone? Thrown out the window for a cute boy she liked to argue with.

He arrived with flowers.

"I don't think anyone has even given me flowers before," she said, accepting them with pleasure. "Ah – come in while I put them in water." She stepped back.

"Obviously you haven't been treated right in the past...I...I mean...ah. Not all guys know how to treat a woman."

Her back was to him so she didn't have to hide her smile, though she checked her laugh.

"I'm sure you can show them how it's done," she said over her shoulder.

The flowers were yellow which made her wonder again if he'd looked at her file where it was listed under "favourite colour". Though why her favourite colour was relevant to her dating life she wasn't sure. She debated whether to say something. She'd never held back with him before so why start now?

"I love the colour, thank you," she began – best not to accuse him outright.

"They reminded me of the dress you wore at the party. You looked so beautiful that night. I mean, you look beautiful now too. You always...look...beautiful."

She filled the vase with water and managed to control the laughter that wanted to bubble out. She turned back to him, carrying the flowers. "It's my favourite colour, thank you."

"It suits you. Not that I know much, or anything, about that sort of thing. Gina is better at that than me. She was always good at art."

"Come on," she ushered him out of the kitchen ahead of her and put the vase on the wonky table in the lounge. He hovered awkwardly near the door and seemed relieved when she suggested they go. He opened the car door for her, something she'd only seen done in movies. She thanked him but didn't make any further comment, to avoid making him stutter again. On the set he had been completely in control, but he was an entirely different person away from work.

"Thank you," he said, once they were seated in the car.

"You're welcome," she said automatically; then, "Wait, what for?"

"Thank you for coming out with me." He clicked his seatbelt into place and started the car. "I know I don't give the best first impression. In fact, I gave you a pretty awful one I'm sure. I wasn't thinking about anything other than work, not how I came across, or my friend's feelings, or yours. Thank you."

Lizzy looked out the window, watching the street pass by in the dark. "Oh, I had no idea you'd take it so seriously."

"I know. You thought I was a corporate drone. A reality TV hack just out for the views. I was just desperately trying to save my show."

"And maybe a little traumatised over what happened to your sister?" she offered, risking a glance at him.

He looked surprised. "I hadn't thought of that. Yes, you're probably right. She's everything I have. What happens to her, when she gets upset – I feel responsible."

"You can't hold yourself responsible, she's an adult."

"This was my show. My choice. My fault. I should have kept a better eye on her, on all the contestants. What George did was not ok. I should have seen what kind of man he was. He gives the rest of us a bad name."

"Not all men, right?"

He cringed. "I've probably said something like that in the past. Gina has lectured me about it."

Lizzy kept playing with her hands; it had been a long time since she'd been on a date and she wasn't sure how to talk to William when she wasn't critiquing him. They were silent until they pulled up at the restaurant.

Something occurred to her as she closed the car door and she said, "But the show must go on?"

William stepped onto the footpath and waited for her to join him before he answered. "There are contracts involved. It's out of my hands. I just have to try to make it as good a show as I can with the shots that we got." He tilted his head towards with restaurant and they walked to the door which he opened for her.

"How are you going to end it?" she asked. "I pretty much blew the whole thing out of the water. You can't have a reality TV dating show without a happy ending."

"It's been done before."

Hadn't Mary said something about that too? Lizzy made a mental note to text her after dinner, maybe during dinner if William went to the bathroom.

"I do like a challenge," he added, then gave the waitress his name for their booking.

He held her chair and as she sat down she said, "is that why you're dating me?"

With a wrinkled brow he asked, "is what why I'm dating you?"

"Because you like a challenge."

He relaxed into his chair and laughed; she didn't think she'd ever heard him laugh before. It *was* possible. She'd like to make him laugh again. "I don't think you're a challenge, I think you're exceptional." Then he seemed to realise what he'd said and picked up his menu, murmuring something about the food.

A smile broke across Lizzy's face, pulling at her cheeks. *Exceptional.* She'd never been called that before. A challenge, yes, but never exceptional. She watched him as he resolutely studied the menu. Did she like him? Did she like him because it had been a long time since she'd dated? Did she like him because he thought she was exceptional?

It was only a first date, too early to be psychoanalysing the whole thing – they might never have another. *What if we never have another?* She followed his example and looked at the menu. After the waitress took their drinks orders they sank back into silence. This wouldn't do.

"This is a nice place." It was Thai; the walls were painted red with a beautiful border in wallpaper and large gold art works hanging on the walls.

He nodded.

Lizzy looked around at the restaurant, which was three quarters full.

"Seems popular."

He pressed his lips together and nodded again.

"It's your turn," she said. "I commented on the restaurant, maybe you could say something about the menu."

"Ah...Do you like to read?"

"No. No, that's not a good starter. I'm sure we read completely different books."

"Then maybe we can compare. You never know, I might surprise you." William raised his eyebrows and smiled, challenging her.

"Let me see. Business books, motivational tomes – but your guilty pleasure is a good crime thriller. Am I right?"

She had to stop herself from laughing at the look on his face. "So, what sort of books do you like to read?" he asked instead.

A giggle escaped her. "I'm right then?"

"You might be. Do I get to guess your reading material now?"

"No fair, you have access to my full personal history and psychological evaluations." She cringed. "Not to mention medical history." Her head wanted to meet the table at the memory of all the information he had access to, all that she'd endured to get on that stupid show just to make her mother happy.

The arrival of their drinks was a happy distraction, one William didn't take advantage of.

"I admit, I do have access to your file. But I haven't read it. I mean, I did read it. Just not recently. I read everyone's files before filming to help get a balanced cast, to know what reactions to expect, what dates they'd enjoy."

"Are you sure you didn't study it in preparation for this evening? I'm kidding, I'm kidding..." She took a gulp of wine. It was fine, she wasn't driving. Besides, she needed the alcohol to calm her nerves.

"Russian literature?" he guessed.

She shook her head.

"Something deep and complex, I'm sure."

She laughed. "Because I'm such a deep and complex character. No. I like cosy mysteries."

William sipped his drink a couple of times then put it back on the table. "I have no idea what that is. Mysteries, yes. Cozzie, no."

"'*Cosy*.' Like warm. They're, hmm, they're safe mysteries. Predictable. Formulaic you might say. Lots of quirky characters, often in a small town. It's usually a series, the main character is female, older than protagonists usually are. Nosy. Probably has a cat. Or crafts. Or bakes. Or all of the above. They keep stumbling across dead bodies and somehow manage to then stumble across the culprit but manage to stay relativity safe the whole time. Oh, and there's usually a love interest. A nice guy. Their relationship doesn't progress across the series, it's safe, it's satisfying. Oh, and no sex." Her eyes widened and she felt her cheeks redden. Why on earth did she end on that note?

"They sound...cosy."

"I read biographies sometimes," she said quickly, wanting to show she did have a brain in her head.

"Ah, I bet those have sex though."

"Did you–did you just make a joke?"

William scratched his head. "Perhaps it wasn't a very good one if you have to ask. Gina says I need to lighten up more."

This admission made her want to make one of her own. "My guilty pleasure is romance. Yes, there's sex. There's something so satisfying about meeting two characters that have all this chemistry and you know they're going to fuck." Her mouth hung open as she realised what she'd just said. She snapped it shut. She felt like she couldn't breathe. It was her honest opinion but she didn't know him well enough to know how he would respond. Perhaps saying 'fuck' was too much. She leaned back in her chair attempting to appear nonchalant. "Unless I accidentally stumble across a sweet romance or heaven forbid a Christian one," she added.

He raised is eyebrows in question.

"Christians don't have sex. Apparently."

"Their numbers would suggest otherwise."

He leant forward, his lips slightly parted; she felt heat between her legs at the expression on his face, and then the waitress came to take their order. He sat back, picked up his menu and gestured for her to order first. Air rushed out of her lungs. They'd just avoided something but she wasn't sure what and she wasn't sure how she felt about it.

"I always get Pad Thai," she said, almost apologetically.

The waitress turned to him but his gaze was locked on Lizzy instead, "I'd like something a little spicy, this curry please." And he glanced down at his menu, pointing.

Lizzy felt like she couldn't breathe again. Was he flirting with her?

**

"I don't know what I was thinking," William said on the drive home. "I shouldn't've had that curry. I don't really like spice."

She laughed. "Then why did you get it?"

"I don't know. I wanted to impress you."

"Oh." She smiled. "I was very impressed. I promise."

"Gina told me to take a risk. This whole thing feels risky. I'm really out of my comfort zone. I don't date often and you're so – you're so..."

"I don't date often either."

"I find that hard to believe."

"Well, it's the truth," she said with a shrug. "My mother thinks I intimidate men. That I should quieten down so I can settle down." She closed her eyes in mortification. "I don't know why I just told you that."

"I don't know why I tell you anything. I look at you and words just come out of my mouth, completely bypassing my brain. Like that, just there. I shouldn't have said that. Now I've made things weird."

She laughed, softly. "Dating someone you actually care about is a wild ride."

"Yeah."

Lizzy cleared her throat. Had they both just admitted to having feelings for each other?

He walked her to the door and they stood awkwardly on the porch.

William raised his hand, opened his mouth, looked like he was about to say something – to reach for her. But he closed his mouth and touched the hair behind his ear instead.

"What was that?" she asked. Knowing exactly what it was.

"Nothing, nothing."

She was going to have to push him. "Shall I say good night and go into my house?" She jerked a thumb over her shoulder. "I'm home now, I can just go."

"I was going to ask if I could kiss you."

Lizzy stepped towards him, closing the gap between them; she placed her hands on his shoulders and leaned in. His open mouth met her closed one – she pulled back and laughed.

"Let's try this again," she suggested. "Start with a closed mouth."

The same thing happened again. She laughed – the laughter continued, if she didn't stop soon it would escalate into hysteria. Worse than that, he might think she was laughing at him. With some effort she brought herself under control.

He didn't seem daunted, just waiting for her to come back to him. Which she did.

The third time she just went with it, allowing her mouth to open under his, their tongues to touch. It was a long time since she'd had a first kiss, a long time since she'd had a kiss at all. She felt the fibre of his suit coat beneath her fingers, a funny thing to notice at this time.

She pulled away again, laughing lightly this time. "That was good."

"Yeah." There was something in his eyes, like he wanted to devour her. It made her feel powerful and terrified all at once, like she could fall into this, into him, lose herself entirely. Where had the mild-mannered William gone? And did she want him to come back?

"I should go," she said. "But I'll see you soon?"

"Yes. I mean no."

She turned back to him.

"I'm going to Christchurch. For work. To look at the first draft of the show." He looked almost guilty and her stomach dropped a little. She knew it would come to this; it had to.

They said their goodbyes and she entered her house. Waiting till she heard his car drive away before she left the front door. She'd never done that before. What had happened to her?

In her dream she and Charles were in a park surrounded by trees in blossom.

"It's so beautiful," she said, then had to duck to avoid a branch.

Charles was having a worse time of it; he was so much taller than her that he had to lean almost double to get under the canopy. Surely this would look ridiculous on film.

Her feet slid under her on the damp ground, but at least the rain was being kept off them by the blossoms above. The branches pressed down further, until she had to double over too. Charles was on his knees, shuffling along.

"Do you want children?" he asked, resembling nothing so much as an overgrown toddler himself.

She placed her hands on her suddenly swelling belly, then she was standing straight again, all alone amongst the flowers. Her child was Jane, a baby she knew would never cry but would grow to resent her the older she got.

William appeared, holding an umbrella which he used to puncture her stomach.

She awoke with a gasp of loss.

**

They were interviewing editors and somehow she had ended up on the interview panel. She'd written the proposal, drafted the advertisement and reviewed the applications – none of which was in her job description – but it felt like being on the interview panel was going a bit far.

"I don't think this is my area of expertise," she'd protested but Denny was determined she see it through.

None of them knew what they were doing. In the past Denny had hired people he knew, or taken recommendations from current staff.

"It's only contract work," Forster explained. "They charge by the hour, we bill by the hour, and if we don't like what they do we can get rid of them easily enough."

That didn't sound precisely fair.

One of the two locals to apply was the English teacher from the girls' college. She seemed eager to get out of the classroom and disappointed that they couldn't offer compelling hours. The next interviews were online huddled around a laptop. Lizzy made a mental note to suggest a screen in the conference room once this was finished.

"I don't know if it's worth it," Lizzy confessed after the third one of these, pulling the laptop towards her and closing the screen. "What's the point in hiring someone if they aren't here? We could hire someone on the internet from anywhere in the world to get this done. I thought it was about the personal touch."

"It was in the proposal we sent you," Forster said to Denny, "as an option." An option Lizzy had argued against including. "There is a certain amount of risk surrounding that but considering the small numbers involved it's a risk we could carry."

"I want to avoid farming our work out to some underpaid teenager in a third world country. I'd like to keep the work local, at least in New Zealand. That's how we built this company. It's one of our values." He held up his hands. "I'm not saying I'm against diversity."

Lizzy sighed. She couldn't fault Denny for not supporting exploitation but there was only one person in the office who wasn't a shade of white. Then again, that did represent the community they worked in. Their town wasn't exactly a metropolis and about twenty years behind the rest of the country; the only people of colour tended to be the seasonal workers from the Islands who came for harvest and the small Māori community focused around the kura kaupapa, the full language immersion school.

She trudged back to her desk still thinking about the diversity issue.

LIZZY: *Did you consider diversity casting for the show?*

As she slumped back in her chair his answer came.

WILLIAM: *I would have preferred a diverse cast*

WILLIAM: *There are a lot of things I would have done differently if I could*

WILLIAM: *Our hands were tied by the type of people who applied*

Lizzy considered that an excuse; if they had wanted diversity, they could have found it. Though it may have ended up being mere tokenism. She rubbed her hands over her face, wishing she could fix all the world's problems. Nothing would change if people kept doing the same thing. An ugly thought entered her head – was this a white saviour complex?

She only had half an hour at her desk to push through some work before the last interview – in person this time. Time got away from her until Denny had to come from the interview room to remind her they were starting.

Entering the room, she was pleasantly surprised to see the candidate was female with short pink hair and subtle piercings. Sure, she was lily white, but at least she was a little different than everyone else in the office. Surely some change was better than no change?

Bright pink lips spread to reveal charmingly crooked teeth. "Kia ora, I'm Kitty." She held out her hand; Lizzy was pleased with her firm handshake. She pushed back the thought that she'd already made a decision. What a silly thing to do, decide on how someone presented themselves and the firmness of their handshake. Kitty gave her a little half smile as she released her hand. Lizzy had the absurd compulsion to giggle.

Throughout the interview Lizzy felt uncomfortable every time Kitty's eyes fell on her. The eye contact was unnervingly direct, though she noted that Kitty was equally direct with Denny and Forster.

Kitty's farewell handshake lingered just a little longer than expected. Denny indicated he'd walk her out while the others stayed in the room to discuss the candidates.

Lizzy rushed back to her desk to collect her notes from the earlier interviews and give herself some breathing space. She was concerned Forster and Denny would want the first man from the video interviews; he was incredibly inexperienced, but talked a good game.

Denny settled himself back in the chair. "I think the choice is clear but let's give them their due and work through each of the interviews in turn."

"George seemed good," Forster began.

"But did you notice how he talked about his team all the time, never what he individually did?" Lizzy interjected. "I didn't come away from his interview confident that he'd done any of the work, maybe just watched it being done." There was something else about him that bugged her but she couldn't quite put her finger on it.

"That's a good point," Denny said. "You could argue he's modest, doesn't like to blow his own trumpet. He's worked in some good places but the experience isn't quite relevant."

"I would kill the second guy, if I had to work with him," Lizzy blurted.

"Oh, come on," Forster said. "He'd be the life of the party."

They both looked to Denny to break the tie. He rubbed his chin. "I see where you're coming from, Forster. He would be good fun but he'd disrupt things in the office, we wouldn't be able to focus on work. More wasted, unbillable hours. It looks like no one else is going to say it so I will. I think we should hire Kitty. She's the obvious choice."

Lizzy blinked. She'd thought she'd have to fight for this.

"She is a little different to the rest of our team," Forster said slowly. "But she has the most relevant experience. She's flexible and didn't seem to be using this as a stepping stone to something else. I didn't get the impression that she'd only stay here till she found something better with more hours."

"As the closest thing we have to any sort of HR resource, I think it's a good idea to reference check before we make a firm decision," Lizzy said. After an internal struggle she suggested they move forward with Kitty and George, then come to a decision once they had the references before them.

"I still think the second guy would be fun," Forster said reluctantly.

"Maybe. But did he need to point out that his current manager is younger than him?" She jabbed a finger at her interview notes. "The way he talked about him came across as petty. The manager *may* have got his job through nepotism, but he still deserves respect. *Maybe* the guy isn't skilled for the job he's been dropped into but we don't know what's really going on." Lizzy let out a breath after this speech, worrying she'd said too much.

Denny nodded. "What stories would he tell if he decides he doesn't like one of us? There's a lack of loyalty."

Lizzy wasn't sure he'd got the point but let it slide and accepted the role of calling the candidates for their reference details when Denny assigned it to her.

"Kia ora, Kitty speaking."

"Kitty, hi, it's Lizzy from Meryton designs."

"Hi, that was quick, I haven't even got home yet." Her laugh was a tinkle down the line with background noise that Lizzy assumed meant she was driving. She wondered if the car was pink like Kitty's hair, for some reason she pictured a convertible imagining her own hair flowing as she sat in the passenger seat.

She attempted to maintain her professionalism. "We were impressed with your interview and we'd like to proceed to reference checking."

"Ah."

Lizzy's heart sank. "Is that going to be a problem?"

"No. Not exactly. Would you accept references from clients? I've never really had a boss, per se."

"Um, you mean like testimonials?"

"Oh, I have a bunch of those I can send you and samples of my work. I did mention I could supply those in my application."

Lizzy nodded, though Kitty couldn't see her, realising that perhaps they should have asked for samples upfront as part of the application process. They did ask for a portfolio when interviewing designers, even if they were recommended. How could she have been so stupid? She'd been thinking more about manufactured drama than real life.

"Would–would you like those?" Kitty asked when Lizzy didn't say anything.

"Oh, yes! Of course! That would be great! I mean, yes, we would like to see those. Could you potentially provide anyone we could talk to as well? Just to, ah, tick the boxes."

"I could do that. I'm driving right now," she said, confirming Lizzy's suspicion, "but I could email the details within the hour. Does that work for you?"

"That's perfect, thanks Kitty."

"You're very welcome, I'm looking forward to working with you."

Lizzy blinked at her confidence. "Me–me too."

She hung up and sat back for a second with a stupid smile on her face. Kitty would certainly shake things up with the boys in the office, if her references checked out.

The call to George required a change of tactic.

"Yo."

"Hello, is this George?"

"Yep."

"Hi George, this is Lizzy, from Meryton Designs."

"Right."

"We talked this morning."

"Right."

"When you interviewed for the editor role."

"Yep."

Perhaps he wasn't in a good position to talk, she surmised from his short answers.

"Is now a good time to talk? I could call back later."

"Nah, now's good."

"Ok. We would like to move you to the next stage in the process. Do you have references and samples you can send me please?"

"Samples?"

"Yes, of your writing so we can assess your style." She rubbed her neck.

"I didn't know I had to do that."

Technically up until the call with Kitty he hadn't, but Lizzy wanted to have comparable data for the two candidates.

"Well...you can decline to provide samples of your writing but it will make the decision more difficult to assess. If you need some time to pull the samples together, it doesn't have to be immediately."

She hung up after George agreed to email his references and sample work by the end of the week. The negotiation had felt more like an argument. Lizzy wondered if he'd have behaved that way if Denny or Forster had called; in the interview it seemed like he had directed his answers to them and ignored her, but it was hard to tell when he was on a screen. Supervising his work could be difficult; he might be running to the boys and talking behind her back. She sighed and rubbed her neck again. She'd tackle that problem if it came to it.

Most of the guys in the office liked her, although they occasionally grumbled when she pushed them to get their timesheets in on time for billing or to behave like grown adults. It could be hard being the only woman in the office sometimes, but she knew the whole place would fall apart without her. Denny was an exceptional designer but lacked practical business skills. She ensured that the business made money – that the bills were paid, that the staff were paid – with some assistance from Forster. Denny might have directed the design work but Lizzy ensured they met timeframes and budgets.

Maybe having another woman in the office, even if it were just for a few hours a week, would make a difference to the culture. Kitty would have the option to work from home though, as it seemed she did on her other jobs.

An email appeared in her inbox from Kitty. There were five sample writing pieces, each with the client outline and an attached testimonial, beautifully presented. The body of the email included two references of former clients and one from a university lecturer – "in case you need something more formal".

The email from George didn't arrive till late Friday afternoon and was brief. He included one reference and had pasted a writing sample into the email. Lizzy blamed herself for not being clearer on their needs and responded immediately, asking for at least one more reference and one more writing sample.

MARY: *Check your email*

Mary didn't have her email so Lizzy had no idea what that was about. She ignored the message, intending to check when she got home. She knew her colleagues didn't care about work and personal time merging together, at least based on their capacity to drink together, but she preferred to at least try to keep things separate. Unlike one of the guys she could see right now, at his desk, swiping as though his life depended on it – or at least his sex life. Texting wasn't as all consuming as email or social media, it was fine.

She'd forgotten about Mary's message till one came from Jane that afternoon.

JANE: *Have you seen the email?*

That explained it. The email must be about the show. She put her phone down and tried to focus on work. After what felt like a very long stretch of time, but was in reality only two minutes, she locked her screen, picked up her phone and left the office. She could check her email while she got air. Just until the end of the block, then she'd check. But her fingers were already unlocking her phone as she exited the lift and walked through the lobby.

The email was straight to the point. The show would go on. It contained the dates and times when the show would screen on the local television network. Attached were images of her captured during the course of filming for her to share on social media. There was a social media strategy too – tools to use, hashtags, businesses to manage it for her, how to manage sponsorship deals when they came her way.

She'd never posted a selfie before but now seemed like the perfect time. Wouldn't it be the right way to start her campaign? Lydia would no doubt have told her what angle to tilt her head, and how to smile, but she just snapped a quick picture and posted the caption, "Me, discovering that it's actually happening. #bagaboyfriend #comingsoon"

She texted Mary back first, it seemed only fair.

LIZZY: *Thanks for the heads up. Got all the info*

Then Jane.

LIZZY: *I can't believe it's actually happening!*

Jane sent her a flurry of messages, documenting her excitement and squealing about how good her photos were.

It wasn't till she was leaving for the day that it occurred to her that there might be someone else who would be interested. First she thought of William, then Gina and, lastly, her mother. She groaned.

LIZZY: *Want to have dinner tonight?*

An hour later she let herself into her mother's house and walked into the kitchen. She hadn't been there since the fateful day when her mother had blindsided her with the announcement that she'd signed Lizzy up for the dating show. The kitchen looked the same but everything felt different.

Her mother was making pasta. "It's almost ready, perfect timing. Can you set the table?"

And it was perfect timing; as Lizzy put glasses of wine for each of them at the table, her mother plated up.

"Now, to what do I owe this honour?" her mother asked as she settled into her seat.

"Mum, you make it sound like I never see you. We had coffee last week." She picked up her fork and began to eat, eager to put this off as long as she could.

"Never's a strong word, dear."

"Hmm, this is good." She swallowed and shovelled another forkful of pasta into her mouth, not really tasting it.

Her mother viewed her through narrowed eyes, picked up her wine glass and sat back in her seat. "I am your mother, you know. I know when something's bothering you. You might as well get it out. I'm not getting any younger."

Lizzy sighed and balanced her fork on the edge of her plate. She picked up her glass and took a sip. "I got an email today," she began, "and I think you may have got one too."

For once her mother didn't fill the silence but merely lifted her eyebrows in question.

"It's from the production company. They're going to screen *Bag a Boyfriend*."

"Well, that's not exactly surprising, we knew it was going to happen eventually. Was there something else?"

"*I* didn't. I thought it might all just blow over. Mum, I'm–I'm worried how I'm going to come across. How *you're* going to come across. How they portray us is out of our hands and I didn't exactly behave...well." She took a gulp of her wine and appreciated the warmth as it spread through her chest.

"Is that all?" Her mother picked up her fork and poked at her food. "I'm sure it'll be fine."

"Did you–did you get the email?"

"I haven't checked," she said her fork hovering in front of her mouth. "Can we eat first?"

Lizzy didn't have much of an appetite. Now that she'd starting thinking about it, she was worried about how her mother would present on screen. About how she herself would be portrayed, to explain away her behaviour in the final episode. She managed to finish her dinner but refused an offer of dessert.

They went into her mother's small office; her mother was the only person she knew who still had a desktop computer – everyone else relied on a laptop or their phone or occasionally their work computer for personal use. It connected to the system in the shop, allowing her mother to send details through to the accountant and order stock when necessary.

"Are you still using that old guy for your accounting?"

Her mother made a noise of agreement as she booted up the computer.

"How would you feel about a woman managing your accounts?"

Her mother twisted around, "Are you offering?"

Lizzy laughed. "No, no. Not me. I met someone on the show. I think you'd really like her. And being a female-run business, it occurred to me that you may like to hire a female specialist. I don't actually have her contact details but I'm sure we could look her up." Hadn't Charlotte said something about getting in contact after the show?

Her mother allowed Lizzy to take her place at the computer. Sure enough, a quick search of "local accountant Charlotte" brought her up. She had obviously got the email too; her page had been branded with an image from the show.

"Oh, doesn't she look lovely? A little plain, to be sure. But she's got brains..."

Lizzy frowned at the use of the word "plain", Charlotte had used it too, she phased out her mother's speech and clicked the Work With Me button.

"Do you want me to write as you or as me?" They agreed that Lizzy would write as herself, on her mother's behalf, and composed Charlotte a short message stating she'd like to stay in contact, offering her number, and adding that her mother was looking for a new accountant, would she be interested?

That done, Lizzy let her mother drive again to pull up her email. She also had the timetable, promotional shots and social media strategy.

"Oh look, Lizzy, they've got the shop's logo on pictures of you. Did yours have that too?"

"I hadn't noticed. I think it might be best if I help you with this bit."

It took a lot of negotiation to get the wording of each post just as her mother liked it, before using a free scheduler to schedule posts for each episode of the show, promoting either Lizzy as stand-in for the business, or the business itself. After another hour they'd updated the website too, though Lizzy had to argue her mother down to using a smaller picture of her, rather than one splashed across the entire home page.

"And once the episode has aired you can put the pictures of Jane and Charles in the store up on the site too. They were very clear that image wasn't to be released till after the episode. I guess it would let people know who was there."

"Lizzy?"

"Hmm?"

"You've put posts up for you right till the last episode." Her mother speared her with her gaze. "Is there anything you'd like to tell me?"

She backed away. "No, no." She shook her head. "Nothing to tell."

"Lizzy, did you *win*? Are you dating that lovely boy?" She leapt out of her seat. "You did, didn't you? That's why I've hardly seen you. Oh, Lizzy!" She threw her arms around her. "I forgive you. You're going to make such beautiful babies."

"Mum, no." She protested and managed to extract herself. With an inward shudder she recalled her dream of carrying Charles' child, 'Jane'. Did her mother really want grandchildren that badly? "You know I'm not allowed..." The NDA was on the tip of her tongue, a perfect excuse but her mother would never stop unless she told her. Surely it would be cruel to drag her mother along like this? With a sigh she placed her hands on her mother's shoulders and guided her back into the chair. "Mum, I don't know how to say this—"

Her mother's hand flew to cover her mouth. "Oh my God, you're engaged."

"Mum, please let me finish." She swallowed, unsure how to continue. "I was at the last episode, it's true. But I didn't – Charles and I aren't together."

"He broke up with you? Oh my darling!" And her mother was attempting to hug her again.

"That's not–that's not what happened, Mum. I dumped him. No, I–I rejected him."

"You tell yourself whatever you need to, darling, it'll be all right."

She was going to know sooner or later, might as well get it out now.

"He chose me, Mum, and I said no. I said no. I didn't want to do it. It didn't seem right. He was a nice guy in a really awkward position and I didn't feel anything for him and I just couldn't."

"You–you said no?"

"I said no. And on that note, it's late, I should be going." She started to back away but her mother's voice halted her.

"Elizabeth!" Years of being her child won out over being an independent woman.

"What, Mum?"

"Don't you 'what' me. You know exactly what, young lady. Come back here and tell me what happened."

Reluctantly she edged back into the room. Her mother was occupying the only chair so she leant against the desk, remembering not to sit on it because of tapu – something she'd learnt as a child and always followed, even behind closed doors. Her mother wouldn't have noticed.

Lizzy sighed and folded her arms. "What—" she screwed up her face. She knew exactly what her mother wanted to know, no point in asking. "Before I say anything please remember that you signed an NDA and cannot talk about anything I tell you."

Her mother grumbled but agreed. Lizzy surveyed her with narrowed eyes before continuing.

"I did get to the last week. To the last bag ceremony. It was just me and Jane. Oh Mum, Jane is gorgeous and not just that, she's sweet. She's so lovely. She's the sort of person that you want to hate but you can't because she's just so God-damned good. She's a genuine person." Lizzy took a deep breath. "And had – has – genuine feelings for Charles. The boyfriend."

Her mother didn't look convinced.

"And I didn't."

Her mother blinked, processing the information. It was so long before she spoke that Lizzy was considering leaving again when she said, "What does that have to do with anything?" in a waspish tone.

"What do you mean 'what does that have to do with anything'? It has everything to do with...everything." Lizzy threw her hands up. "The production made Charles choose me rather than Jane, I could see it happening and since then William has confirmed that he did, in fact, do that." She pressed her lips together, hoping her mother hadn't noticed that she mentioned another man, she attempted to breeze past it. "The production has confirmed they planned for him to choose me and it just didn't seem right. Jane cares for him, I don't. He should be with Jane." Forestalling her mother's next objection she added, "I mean, as far as I could see he liked her too, it wasn't a one-sided thing."

"You rejected a perfectly good—"

"Guy who wasn't interested in me. Yes." She took a deep breath then said the thing she'd been really worried about. "I don't know how it's going to come across on screen. They could paint me as the villain, the heartbreaker. I don't know if you'll want the shop's name associated with me."

Promotion

Lizzy let herself back into her house, her mother's admonitions still ringing in her ears. She realised she hadn't messaged Mary to thank her properly.

LIZZY: *Thanks. My mother got an email too. Just set up all her social media. Do you need help with yours?*

Mary texted back as she was climbing into bed.

MARY: *I've got a handle on it but I bet Lydia will out do us all*

Charlotte messaged the next day; she had set up her social media too and was willing to take the shop on as a client. Two birds, one stone.

A week later the press releases came out and everything changed. William was back by this point but because of the publicity they had to be careful not to be seen together in public. Which meant their dates were chaperoned by Gina at the vineyard.

"Aren't you breaking the rules?" Gina asked, as they sat at a candlelit table enjoying a roast together.

William made a show of looking around. "I don't see the media anywhere."

It was a lame joke but Lizzy laughed; he needed the encouragement. He grinned back at her.

"Isn't it in your contract that you can't date the..." she gestured at Lizzy, "...talent?"

He looked thoughtful for a moment. "It's not, but it probably should be. I'll be sure to add that if we ever do another season."

“Is that on the cards?” Lizzy asked, aghast.

“Probably not, after the mess these two productions were.”

Lizzy and Gina both winced; they each felt responsible for their season imploding. While Lizzy thought hers was justified, she placed all the blame of Gina’s season at George’s feet. They glanced at each other and shared sympathetic smiles. William continued to eat, appearing completely unaware of how his words had affected them.

After dinner they cleared the table, then Gina excused herself so Lizzy and William could make out on the couch.

“I feel a little like a teenager,” Lizzy confessed.

“You’re all woman to me,” William said, leaning in.

She laughed. “No, I mean, hiding away, no one knowing. Did you ever date someone you weren’t supposed to?”

“I am not revealing my work secrets,” he said with a smile and kissed her.

**

“So, you’re famous,” Kitty said, coming to lean against Lizzy’s desk. It was her first day and Lizzy was thrilled she’d accepted the job.

“Wha... I’m not sure that’s ... Who told you?” She scanned the desks, none of the guys were looking. She dropped her voice. “Did *they* tell you?”

Kitty’s laugh was bright and not at all derisive. “I may have been internet stalking you.” She paused. “And I just now realise I admitted that out loud.” She glanced down at the floor but recovered quickly, meeting Lizzy’s gaze.

Lizzy flapped a hand. "I stalked you before we hired you. Found the blog you kept in high school, your crafting obsession, as well as your professional work."

"Good, good," Kitty nodded, "so long as we're even."

"'Even' might be taking it a bit far. Teenage angst is nothing to total public humiliation." She buried her face in her hands. "I don't know why I did it. It just got so ... messy. I can't ... " her hands dropped and she straightened her shoulders. "I can't talk to you about it, I'm under an NDA." Not to mention she was at work, Kitty was just so much easier to talk to than the guys. She turned back to her computer and shifted paper on her desk, trying to look busy.

Kitty took the hint and started to back away. "Just so long as you know, I'm following you, well, I plan to follow you, because you're a public figure now and I'm ready for the drama. Might follow the others too." She had only taken one step before she swung back around to add, "I'm available for viewing parties. Hashtag friends for life."

Lizzy couldn't help but smile and pulled out her phone to text Mary, Charlotte and Jane. A viewing party sounded like a great idea. If they could get away with not inviting Lydia and Caroline. It was high time she started a group chat.

The group chat had blown up by the time she returned home from work, with enthusiastic talk about a viewing party.

LIZZY: *I'd like to invite a friend from work. But I don't know if it should just be us?*

Using the word friend was pushing it but Lizzy thought Kitty could easily transition from colleague into friend.

JANE: *I'd love to meet your friend!*

JANE: *If it's ok with everyone else*

MARY: *Viewing parties with friends are traditional. She could be our groupie*

Charlotte put her two cents in several hours later.

CHARLOTTE: *Sorry, just catching up. Work*

CHARLOTTE: *Should we give ourselves a name?*

CHARLOTTE: *A group name*

MARY: *Charlie's Angels – too on the nose?*

CHARLOTTE: *The more the merrier L. Invite your friend too*

JANE: *Charlie's Angels is perfect*

LIZZY: *We cannot get any cheesier can we?*

She changed the name of the group chat to Charlie's Angels, wondering what Charles would think if he ever found out. As she was getting into bed she discovered Mary had already started using the name as a hashtag; seemed like this wasn't going to be an inside joke.

Broadcasting

Episode One

Appropriately Kitty turned up with pink wine; she eyed Jane and the kiss she gave Lizzy when she arrived.

"Do you and Jane have a thing?" Kitty whispered as she uncorked the wine.

Lizzy blinked at her and handed her wine glasses.

"Do you like her? Are you involved?" Kitty prompted.

"Oh! Oh. No. Jane's, she's, well she's far too pretty to be interested in someone like me—"

"I'm sure that's not—"

"—and besides, I'm pretty sure she's straight. And into someone. I don't know if it's going to work out but, yeah. I can't ...tell you." Lizzy wanted to mention the NDA that kept her lips sealed but mentioning it was just as good as screaming that Jane was hung up on Charles. Somewhere in the back of her mind was an echo about protesting too much.

Kitty nodded. "So who else is coming? Other contestants?"

"Ah yeah," Lizzy said relieved, "Mary and Charlotte."

"What about Lydia and Caroline?"

"Do you know everyone who was involved?"

Kitty shrugged. "What can I say? I'm an excellent internet stalker. Not like it's hard, you're using the same hashtags."

"We're not..." Lizzy stopped herself from saying Lydia and Caroline weren't friends of hers. That may have been covered by the NDA too, and if not might make her look bad. "I'm closest with Jane. And Charlotte. And Mary."

"So, one of the other two was the bitch in the group; I get you, I know how these things go. It'll be fun trying to work out who. I hope it wasn't Lydia, we've been vibing in her comments."

Lizzy pressed her lips together to keep from saying anything; perhaps inviting Kitty had been a bad idea, they'd all need to keep a lid on behind the scenes secrets.

Mary was next to arrive. As she accepted a glass of wine from Kitty her eyes kept flicking up to her hair. "I feel a theme going on," she said eventually in an even tone.

"Pink was my favourite colour growing up," Kitty said. "But then I rejected it as too girly. What a ridiculous notion! To hate something that once made you happy because of internalised misogyny."

Mary's face lit up as she recognised a compatriot. "Fuck the patriarchy." She offered her glass with a tilt of her head.

"Fuck the patriarchy," Kitty repeated and their glasses clinked.

Lizzy left them to it, knowing they'd be caught up in their feminist agenda. The night rang, on and off, with their occasional outbursts of "Fuck the patriarchy!"

"*Key chain on the ground*," Jane sang softly.

"What?"

"Taylor Swift," Jane said, as though that explained everything. "Are any of your other friends coming, Lizzy?" she asked as she sat beside her on the couch.

Lizzy shook her head. "I wouldn't have invited anyone without checking." They were silent for a moment sipping the wine. Something occurred to her. "I'm not sure I *have* friends."

"Lizzy, I'm sure you have plenty of friends."

"I *had* friends, but they moved away or got married and had kids, and I never see them anymore." It was a slightly depressing thought that, prior to the show, her life had consisted of work and seeing her mother. "I guess I should be grateful to my mother for talking me...no, *guilting* me, into this whole thing. God, I really needed a shake up."

Jane patted her knee. "Well, you have me now and I'm not going anywhere."

"Not even if Charles showed up on a white charger and swept you off your feet?"

"Lizzy, we're talking about actual possibilities. Charles had his chance with me." She blinked rapidly as though she was holding back tears.

"You never did go into detail about what happened between you two after I left."

Jane shook her head then Lizzy was distracted by the arrival of Charlotte who apologised for being late, she'd been caught up at work. As they'd agreed to meet quarter of an hour early so they could catch up, Charlotte's timing was perfect to grab a glass of wine – "interesting shade" – and a seat before the show started.

"This is it! This is it!" Kitty said, bouncing from her place on the floor in front of Mary's chair – Lizzy had offered her a chair from the table but she had refused. Proximity to the snacks on the coffee table was her explanation.

An advert started the show, followed by another, and then another.

"Is it ever going to get to the good part?" Mary asked.

"I'm not sure there *is* a good part," Charlotte said, hushing the end of her sentence as Bill Lucas filled the screen.

The man himself was a walking advertisement, mentioning his own business regularly, along with several of the sponsors including the travel agency who had provided the grand prize. "Apart from love, of course!" Finally they were in the ballroom again. The set-up looked less awkward, less artificial and more intimate on screen than it had been in person.

The room chorused with each contestants' name as they were introduced – Jane blushed as the others added how gorgeous she looked, which she did. Charles came across better than expected too; endearingly shy rather than bumbling.

Lizzy couldn't help but glance at Jane to see her reaction to the first meeting with Charles but she seemed to be bearing it well.

This episode was the longest, due to the introductions and Charles having all six contestants to date. Lydia had a cooking date with Charles but she was more interested in touching him and trying to pour alcohol down his throat, someone had helped her procure tequila and she was intent on using the lemon from their lemon meringue pie for shots. When they said goodbye she kissed him and the room whooped in appreciation. Caroline kissed him with more finesse during an art gallery date.

"That date would've been completely boring if she hadn't kissed him," Mary declared during the ad break. "I enjoy art but they should focus on activity dates." She shifted in her seat during her own date, bowling, but remained silent.

Mary was the first to speak when the credits rolled. "It felt a little rushed, if I'm being honest."

"You left on the first episode!" Kitty cried.

"I know, I mean the episode felt rushed. They should have done one that was purely introductions like they do on *The Bachelor*. You know, everyone walks the carpet, does something stupid or says something stupid, they all drink too much and at the end of the night he keeps the girls whose names he remembers or who haven't insulted him."

Charlotte got up to refill her wine. "Does anyone else want some?" There were several raised glasses. "You're not wrong," she said when she sat back down, "about them needing an introductory episode. The problem, of course, is that how could they get that sponsored? You can see how heavy-handed they are with their promotions. What were they going to do – have us wear sandwich boards?"

"I wouldn't put it past them," Lizzy said. "I'm surprised only you and I are were sponsored by a specific business. Considering how things turned out I would have thought everyone would be."

"I don't think they had many applicants," Jane said. "They kept asking me if I had friends who would want to do the show with me. They called it a 'bonding experience.'"

"Yeah," Lizzy said. "Cos fighting over the same guy is a great way to bond."

"They wanted us all to look as good as you," Mary put in, "which is part of the reason I voted myself out at the first opportunity."

Jane waved Mary's comment away. "You're pretty, Mary."

Mary saluted her with her wine glass. "Thank you, but I cannot hold a candle to you."

Kitty nodded enthusiastically, then seemed to realise what she was saying about her new best friend and stopped.

"I'm looking forward to seeing how this whole thing unfolds," Mary said with a significant look at Lizzy.

**

At some point during the next day Kitty was added to the Charlie's Angels chat group. Lizzy suspected Mary was the culprit, but as they'd all got along so well the night before she didn't protest.

KITTY: *I feel like I'm hanging out with celebrities*

MARY: *You're one of us now!*

MARY: *Though, technically, I suppose you should also date Charles*

MARY: *Does anyone know how to get in touch with Charles?*

KITTY: *I want to be one of the cool kids but Charles is the wrong gender for me*

The chat showed Jane typing for several minutes before her message came through.

JANE: *Maybe we could do a reunion?*

MARY: *I apologise for my hetero-normative assumption*

Lizzy exhaled slowly. Jane was still hung up on Charles. Should she get his details and try to organise a reunion? Would it be harmful to Jane rather than helpful? If Charles had really cared for her, he would have chosen her rather than be influenced by William.

She text Kitty separately to apologise for her own "hetero-normative assumption" – after she'd googled exactly what that meant.

LIZZY: *Sorry, I didn't realise you're gay. Is gay an ok word to use?*

KITTY: *I've been flirting with you since I met you*

Lizzy blinked at the message, unsure how to respond. Should she respond at all?

KITTY: *I'm not too hung up on labels*

KITTY: *Maybe I'm not as good as flirting as I thought I was?*

LIZZY: *I feel like maybe you're doing it now?*

KITTY: *Bingo!*

Lizzy smiled. She enjoyed the banter with Kitty – which she now identified as flirting. Was it ok to continue when she didn't intend it to go anywhere? She filed that one away to talk to Kitty about in person – that was going to be an awkward conversation. Maybe she'd been giving off vibes; now Kitty's question about her relationship with Jane made sense.

The rest of Saturday morning she spent cleaning her house, before deigning to make an afternoon appearance at her mother's shop.

"Darling, in the future, can you let me know when you're coming so I can let all my peeps know?"

"Peeps?"

"My people. My public." She pulled a face. "*Your* public. It's not much use to me having you visit if no one knows you're here."

"Nice to see you too, Mum."

"Now that I know how to use the social media I've got everyone signing up. All anyone's wanted to talk about all morning is the show."

"Has it positively impacted sales? I mean, that was the whole point." She looked around the now empty store.

"Fudge has been selling well, everything else...not so much." Her mother sighed. "It has always been my best seller."

Could the store stay afloat on fudge and social media?

**

"You know Kitty?"

"I do not know Kitty personally, no. I have heard you mention her, however, as a colleague." It was William, of course. Who else would talk like that?

They were hiding at his house again, after dinner. Gina had left them on the couch. William was sitting straight while Lizzy had her back against the arm of the couch, her legs on the cushions and her feet tucked under William's legs.

Lizzy scrunched her face. "Work friend."

"My apologies, work *friend*. That's quite a distinction."

"She, um... came to our viewing party of the first episode and we're inviting her to all the others, she's become one of the girls."

After a moments silence William asked, "Did she enjoy it?"

"Obviously, or she wouldn't want to come back."

"I'm glad she's transitioned from work colleague to work friend – or perhaps we can drop the 'work' part of the title?" He leaned forward to pick up his wine glass from the coffee table, his weight shifting on Lizzy's feet.

"She's a lesbian," Lizzy blurted. William's wine glass froze half-way to his mouth. "I think," she added.

William nodded, took a sip of his wine and placed his glass back on the table. Lizzy found she couldn't look at him and instead played with the tassels on one of the pillows.

"Does this," William spoke slowly as though carefully choosing his words, "bother you? It–you don't seem like the kind of person this would bother." He placed the hand nearest her on her ankle. When she didn't answer he spoke again. "I know this is a small town that...perhaps you might be tainted—"

"*Tainted?* Tell me what you really think!" She drew back her feet, hugging her knees.

"Lizzy, I don't care that your friend is a lesbian," he burst out, turning his whole body towards her, "but it seems like you do, and honestly that makes me wonder if you are who I thought you were."

Lizzy blinked back sudden tears at his raised voice. Unless she'd started yelling first, she never dealt well when men raised their voices; it reminded her of her father.

"Oh God, Lizzy, I'm sorry. I didn't mean to make you cry." William dropped to the floor next to her, kneeling in supplication – it seemed like he wanted to put his arms around her but wasn't sure if his advance would be repelled. He patted her knee softly. "I'm sorry, I'm so sorry. Please talk to me. Please look at me."

With great effort Lizzy wrenched her gaze from the back of the couch to look at William through her tears. She blinked, sniffed, and wiped her eyes.

"So," he said gently, "Kitty is a lesbian." He looked at her expectantly.

"I think she might like me." Lizzy let out a sob and put her head on her knees. William's hand stroked her back now.

"Is that such a bad thing? What's not to like?"

"I think," she said from within her cocoon, "I might like her too."

William's hand stilled on her back and Lizzy raised her face to look at him.

"Hey," he said. "It's not a bad thing to like someone." He blinked rapidly. "Is it – have you not been attracted to a woman before?"

Lizzy shook her head and her face crumpled again.

"Hey, hey, it's ok." William put his arms around her, curled up knees and all. He kissed her hair. "It's ok. There is nothing wrong with being attracted to someone of the same sex." His chest rose in a deep breath Lizzy felt against her side. "It's a...time of discovery for you. I'm honoured that you'd share this with me."

When William released her Lizzy noticed him wiping his own eyes. He tipped the rest of his wine down his throat before resuming his former seat on the opposite end of the couch. Slowly, Lizzy stretched her legs back out till her feet were touching his thighs. He glanced down and patted her feet but couldn't seem to raise his eyes to her face.

He got up again and picked up his empty wine glass. "Well, it's getting late." With a nod he moved towards the kitchen.

Lizzy drained her own wine and followed him.

He helped her into her coat and held her tight. "Thank you, our time together has meant so much to me."

Lizzy pulled back. "I don't want to break up with you." It was a statement, not a plea.

"What? I thought that's why you..." William ran a hand through his hair. "I'm confused. I thought you liked Kitty."

"I do. I mean, I think I do. But that doesn't mean I don't like you – still."

"Well...We never discussed the parameters of our relationship—"

"Parameters?"

"We haven't agreed on being exclusive—"

"Are you seeing someone else?"

"No."

"Well, good."

"But that doesn't mean that you couldn't."

"What?"

William scratched his neck and spoke to the ceiling. "Because of my work I don't have traditional relationships, mostly long-distance. So I've never expected my partners to remain faithful – no, that's the wrong word. We agreed we would be together when we were, but were able to...explore other opportunities when apart."

"Are you in a long-distance relationship right now?"

"Well no," he gestured at her, "you're right in front of me. But I feel like I'm not expressing myself well." He took her hands. "I want you to be happy. I would like to make you happy. But what if there's someone else that could make you happy too? I've never – I've never told anyone how I conduct my relationships in the past for fear of stigma but maybe it's time that I start...allowing – no, wrong word again..."

"You want me to date Kitty?"

"If that's what you want."

"And still date you?"

"If that's what you want," he repeated.

**

Lizzy was a little bewildered by this encounter. It played through her head as she drove home. When she arrived, there was a series of texts from William.

WILLIAM: *I'm sorry I made you cry*

WILLIAM: *And then pushed you out the door*

WILLIAM: *I don't always deal with things well*

WILLIAM: *I thought you were breaking up with me*

WILLIAM: *Of course, you're allowed to break up with me, I didn't want to get upset in front of you*

Lizzy allowed herself the smile at his vulnerability that she wouldn't have were he in front of her. She could almost see his brain ticking over and was reasonably sure he'd also be upset with himself for sending the messages.

LIZZY: *We're not breaking up. Everything is fine. Good night*

She worried for a moment that was too short then followed it with a series of emojis.

**

The week passed as weeks often did, with Lizzy chasing the designers to finish their paperwork and timesheets, interspersed with occasional chats with Kitty and evenings surveying the day's conversation on the group chat.

LIZZY: *I'm happy to host again unless we want to rotate?*

KITTY: *I live in a studio, you wouldn't fit*

LIZZY: *Just checking we do want to have a viewing party again?*

Several messages with "yes" followed then Kitty sent a string of emojis.

JANE: *Of course. I love seeing you all and I don't want to watch alone. I'm not comfortable seeing myself on the TV*

Not for the first time, Lizzy wondered if Jane might be harbouring some body image issues that the others had overlooked. It was too easy to assume someone so beautiful wouldn't have any doubts in that area. How had Jane coped with modelling? But of course, she hadn't, that was why Jane worked with children rather than cameras. Lizzy recalled all the paperwork and assessments she'd undergone before the show. If there had been anything serious, surely Jane would have been weeded out at that point? An ugly thought intruded, reminding her how good Jane looked on camera, and how the show may have cared more about that than her wellbeing. She made a mental note to check on Jane after each show – now she had another thing to worry about, not just that Jane may still be hung up on Charles.

Episode Two

Mary was the first one to arrive and confessed she was more interested in watching now that she'd left the show.

"You told me what happens at the end," she told Lizzy, "but I don't know what happens in between. Or how they're going to play it. They always try to mislead. Since it was you and Jane at the end they'll try to play up the relationship between her and Charles."

Lizzy bit her lip; she had always thought there was more going on between Jane and Charles in the first place – there wouldn't be much to "play up". She was saved from answering by Charlotte's arrival.

"I was determined not to be late this week. Especially as it's my week."

Mary made a noise of disappointment. Charlotte looked concerned.

"You've ruined it for her," Lizzy explained. "She didn't know you left next."

Charlotte called out her apologies and followed Lizzy into the kitchen for a drink.

"What's up?" Charlotte asked. "You've got a 'I want to say something but I'm not sure about it' look on your face."

"You're too good at that." Lizzy reached into the upper cupboard for the wine glasses. "I had an...interesting interaction this week."

"Is everything ok at work?"

Lizzy assured her that it was.

"Did someone recognise you from the show?"

She shook her head and glanced at the clock on the wall. She sighed, realising if she was going to tell Charlotte it had to be now, before everyone else arrived.

"Kitty is a lesbian."

"Yes, I picked up on that. Also, she told us on the group chat."

"Right, right." She busied herself pouring wine.

"Does this bother you?" Charlotte prodded, sounding remarkably like William.

Lizzy shrugged. "No. I think maybe I like her." She took a deep breath then rushed on. "But I'm kinda seeing someone else and when I told him he said he'd be ok with me dating her too and I don't know how I feel about that and I've seen Kitty at work but not in a, you know, private context since I had that conversation."

Charlotte nodded and accepted a glass of wine. "If you're asking for advice, I'm not sure I'm qualified to give any. I'm ace." Seeing the look of confusion on Lizzy's face she continued, "I'm asexual, I'm not interested in sex. And possibly aromantic – which means I'm not into romance either. I am *theoretically* interested in romance but it's very rare for me to feel anything. Which is why it was so easy for me to go on the show."

Lizzy nodded, her mind reeling, and led the way back to the lounge. She handed Mary her glass and hovered for a moment.

"If this whole thing," she gestured at the TV, "is about the patriarchy does it have something to do with our relationship with our fathers?"

Mary opened her mouth but there was a knock at the door, saving Lizzy from a lecture and potentially having to face her demons.

Kitty and Jane arrived one after the other, both giving Lizzy enthusiastic hugs which made her question her feelings for both of them.

"Do *not* spoil it for Kitty," Mary demanded, waving her arms at all assembled, as they settled themselves in the lounge. "She's the only one who doesn't know what happens."

Jane mimed zipping her lips up as the show started.

"Are you ok?" Kitty leaned towards Lizzy to ask quietly during one of the ad breaks. "You seem a little quiet tonight. Actually, you've been quiet all week. Is the pressure of fame too much for you?" Her face changed from concern to teasing.

"I'm fine. I'm just...working through some things. Can I, ah," she took a deep breath, "talk to you about it later? Could you stay at the end?"

Kitty nodded.

Lizzy could hardly focus on the rest of the show. Unable to believe that she had committed to having the conversation with Kitty, she fidgeted her way through the rest of the hour. She was almost surprised that Charlotte was sent home then she recalled several reshoots of the final scene and saying goodbye to her outside the hotel.

Kitty turned to Charlotte as the credits rolled. "Oh, Charlotte."

Charlotte shrugged. "From here on out I'm in the same boat as you. It's all a surprise. I'm looking forward to it. Sure, the heavy-handed advertising isn't great but the people part is interesting." Lizzy wondered whether she saw them as some sort of scientific experiment, observing the feelings that were foreign to her. Perhaps it wasn't so different from how Mary dissected the show.

"Don't worry, I'll help clean up," Kitty declared and began ushering everyone out the door. Charlotte shot Lizzy a look and waited for Lizzy to nod before complying.

Kitty seemed to be waiting for Lizzy to start talking but she was putting it off. She realised how much more awkward it would be to have the conversation with nothing to distract her, looking directly at Kitty, so she pushed herself to start talking while she washed the wine glasses. Because wearing rubber gloves was so sexy.

"So." She cleared her throat. "You said something that... No."

Kitty put a hand on her shoulder, which did not help Lizzy to calm down. "It's ok, take your time."

"I think I might like you," Lizzy said aggressively to the sink.

"Oh, wow," Kitty's hand left her shoulder and Lizzy felt her move away. "I'm flattered. Obviously. You're gorgeous and funny and..."

Lizzy turned to find Kitty leaning against the bench.

"I'm kinda seeing someone," Kitty finished. "And I thought you were into Jane."

Lizzy placed a glass on the drying rack and dropped the brush back in the sink. "I think I might be," she confessed, amazed to hear herself speak the words out loud. "But it's complicated. I'm pretty sure she's straight, I don't even *know* what I am and I'm kinda seeing someone else too." She tried to fold her arms, then remembering the wet rubber gloves, stopped herself. "He's great and he said he doesn't mind me dating other people, he's been really accepting about the whole thing. Not what I expected."

"People can surprise you." Lizzy knew Kitty meant her own declaration. "My thing is kinda new. I'm trying not to get too caught up in it. I'm not...good at maintaining boundaries when I'm in a relationship. I can lose myself to them. I don't want to do that this time. She's – she's so much fun and she's so vibrant." Kitty's whole face lit up.

Something like disappointment mixed with relief settled in Lizzy's stomach, then came embarrassment. "That was... yeah, I said some things I now wish I hadn't. I hope that this doesn't make things awkward between us? Here, or at work." She turned back to the sink and picked up the last dirty wine glass.

"It doesn't change anything between us," Kitty assured her. "Hell, if you'd said something before I...Yeah, no."

Lizzy felt a smile pull across her face. "If things go south with that girl, you come find me."

Kitty laughed and picked up a glass to dry. "It's a deal."

Episode Three

"Heading into Week Three," Kitty said in a commentator voice from her seat on the floor in front of Mary, "we have Lizzy, Jane," she pointed at them each in turn, "and Lydia and Caroline still in the race to win Charles' heart. Who will go home this week disappointed?"

Lizzy and Jane smiled at each other.

"I'm so excited," squealed Mary. "I kinda know what happens but I don't know the middle bit, the meat of the story."

"I have no idea what happens. I'm interested to see where this goes. Can they possibly shove one more heavy-handed promotion into the show?" Charlotte said dryly.

There was quickly muffled laughter as the show started with the usual long series of product placements, then Bill Lucas' face filled the screen.

"Oh, I missed you this ceremony Charlotte," Lizzy said quietly, as the screen panned to the ladies arranged in the ballroom for the bag ceremony. "You stood right next to me, then you were gone."

Charlotte gave her a warm smile, then turned back to the television as Bill's voiceover announced the first date of the evening. They may not have had a confession camera but Caroline was speaking her mind to Charles at every opportunity, as he became more and more uncomfortable.

"Wow, she does *not* like you Lizzy," Mary commented after one of Caroline's barbs.

Lizzy shrugged. "I don't think she likes anyone." After a moment she added, "probably least of all herself." Several faces turned to look at her, she smiled innocently back, raised her glass in a salute and took a sip of wine. She barely drank in a normal week, but the screening nights she'd been having a couple of glasses, followed by a couple of glasses when she had dinner with Gina and William. Perhaps it was time to cut back.

She switched to water in the ad break while assuring Jane that she was fine, Caroline's comments hadn't really hurt her. After the break it was Jane's turn to have her date with Charles. It was almost painful to see them together. Lizzy knew they'd have to play up Jane's relationship with Charles to make it a surprise when she was picked instead, but it was probably a more accurate portrayal of what happened than her own scenes with him. It was all there.

In her periphery she watched Jane, who seemed to somehow make herself smaller as she watched herself on screen, occasionally glancing away as though it was too painful to watch. Lizzy put a hand on her arm and murmured, "you know, we don't have to watch this if you don't want to."

Jane gave her a grateful smile and shook her head. After that she didn't seem as affected, she relaxed in her seat rather than pressing herself into the corner. Lizzy worried she might just be hiding it better.

Lydia's date consisted of a drive in an expensive hired car and her trying to tempt Charles into the back seat.

"They used a drone to film this," Mary said knowledgeably as a sweeping view of the car driving down a country road filled the screen.

Lizzy's date didn't seem much altered, apart from them obviously cutting all the waiting around and sound checks. She'd forgotten that this was the day she kissed Charles. There they were under the blossoms and on camera it seemed so natural, it seemed like *he* had been the one to kiss *her*.

"Oooh," filled the room from all sides. Lizzy hid herself behind a cushion, Jane patted her arm.

She emerged to watch the bag ceremony and the exit of -

"Lydia!" shrieked Kitty as Lizzy became Charles' last choice and Lydia had to leave. "She never—" She stopped herself, looked around the room. "I'm just surprised, I thought it would be Caroline leaving."

"She makes the drama," Charlotte said. "She makes good TV. As much fun as Lydia is..." she shrugged.

They watched as Charles led Lydia out. There were gasps as she tried to kiss him, *really* kiss him. Lizzy noticed that Kitty seemed particularly perturbed by this; she meant to ask her why but after the credits rolled and the mess was cleaned up and the goodbyes said, she forgot.

Episode Four

"I both want to know who leaves this week but at the same time I *don't* want to know," confessed Charlotte as they gathered once again in Lizzy's lounge, all in their regular spots; Charlotte on a chair, Lizzy and Jane on the couch together, Mary on the chair across from Charlotte with Kitty on the floor at her feet. "I can't believe next week is the final."

There was murmured assent from around the room.

"The whole thing only took a week to shoot," Jane said. "But it felt like a lifetime. Then again, it feels like a lifetime ago." She smiled weakly and shrugged. Lizzy patted her arm, knowing she was thinking of Charles.

"I'm going to make a bet," Kitty declared, "that Caroline wins. We see each other every week, we text most days, I don't think any of you would be capable of keeping a boyfriend secret from the rest of us. So, I think Caroline wins." She nodded and folded her arms.

Mary looked at Lizzy as she spoke, "I don't want to spoil anything for you, Kitty – or Charlotte – but I...You know what? I don't think I can say anything *without* spoiling it so I'm just going to shut up." She pressed her lips together and leaned back in her chair; Kitty absently patted her knee.

Hmm, perhaps Mary was the woman Kitty was seeing. But just like the possibility of them hiding a boyfriend, it seemed unlikely that the pair of them could hide that from the group. And why would they? It's not like they were dating the producer. Kitty noticed Lizzy watching them and smiled, raising her eyebrows in question. Lizzy shook her head and turned her attention to the TV, where the show had thankfully started.

Lizzy cringed during her date, listening to herself hope she didn't throw up from eating undercooked seafood. "I didn't get sick," she assured the room.

Funny how now she was remembering William hovering in the background clearer than Charles who had been right in front of her at the time.

"Caroline had this theory," she said in the ad break before the bag ceremony, "that the last date of the day was cursed. Whoever went on the last date was the person that left. This day, I had the last date." She leaned back into the couch as Kitty gasped.

"Did you survive?"

"I can't tell you that! Besides, you'll see in a minute."

The room was tense as the show restarted – "Get off the screen Billy-boy, no one cares!" Kitty squealed – then it was the girls on one side of the ballroom with Charles on the other side.

Jane was called first.

"Yes!" came quietly from Charlotte; she gave an embarrassed smile to Jane.

"I cannot bear the tension," Kitty said; she and Mary were holding hands tightly. "Why do they have to draw it out so much?"

"Lizzy," Charles said, and there was a collective sigh of relief from the watching room.

Caroline stalked across the television screen.

"I did not want him to pick that Caroline, she rubs me up the wrong way," Kitty said.

Charlotte turned to the pair on the couch. "That means it's the two of you in the final. This whole time you've been sitting next to each other and it's been the two of you. You're not fighting or anything."

Jane put her head on Lizzy's shoulder. "Nope," she said simply.

Lizzy had an urge to put an arm around Jane, to kiss her hair, but pushed those down. She wasn't sure if they were purely platonic.

**

The week leading up to the final was a frenzy. The local populace had finally jumped on the publicity train. Both Lizzy and Jane were interviewed by the paper and the radio – each trying to trip them up. Jane, with studied softness, deftly avoided each question while Lizzy joked with the interviewers that if she told them she'd have to kill them, kill herself or be killed by the big bad corporation for violating her NDA.

"Did you really have to say that?" William asked. "They contacted me for a comment as they know I'm based locally; the rest of the production team get off scott-free."

Gina said something in the background and William groaned then, in a muffled voice – he'd tried to put his hand over the phone – Lizzy heard him say, "I am *not* in love with her."

Lizzy smirked. "You know there's such a thing as mute button," she offered when his attention returned to her.

"Please tell me you didn't hear that."

"Hear what?"

“What my sis—Oh, thank you.” After a moment he added, “Did you want to watch the final together? I understand this may be hard for you.”

“I appreciate the offer but I don’t want to disappoint the girls. Before you say anything, if I invite you then I’ll have to explain you. They were contestants, they’ll recognise you.”

“Of course, of course. Dinner then? Same time, same place? I want to make the most of the time I have with you. I have to leave on that job next week.”

Lizzy pressed her lips together. She wasn’t sure how to word this. “And we’re still – you’re ok if...I...see other people?”

“If that’s what you want,” he replied cautiously. “If you’d rather I didn’t see other people, I’m happy not to. Honestly, I spend so much of my time thinking about you I’m not really sure there’s...” He seemed to catch himself and cleared his throat.

Episode Five

The final episode was just as long as the previous ones even though there were only two of them left. Lizzy was pleased her spa date was treated respectfully, at least on screen.

"Take it off," Kitty squealed at the on screen Lizzy holding the robe closed up to her throat.

Lizzy threw a cushion at her.

Jane's final date was a picnic at a flower farm. The fields covered in colourful blossoms was a beautiful backdrop but the eagerly anticipated kiss never came.

They each spoke about the sponsors prior to the bag ceremony with their thoughts on Charles squeezed in. Finally, it was the closing ceremony.

Lizzy had vague recollections of standing there, Jane's hand in her own, but having an out of body experience, like all of this was happening to someone else.

"Lizzy."

She jerked in her seat, as startled as she had been the first time when Charles spoke her name.

There was utter silence in the room, eyes flicked to her then back to the screen. Mary and Jane knew what had happened next, but Kitty and Charlotte didn't – they didn't know the disaster that was coming. Jane grasped her hand, just like she had that fateful night.

Lizzy's breathing was rapid. Here it came.

But instead of showing Lizzy's rejection of Charles and her dramatic departure, Bill Lucas appeared on screen. He looked a little flustered, his face sweaty, his eyes moving a little too quick, but only enough that you'd notice if you were really looking.

"Jane, I'm sorry, that means your journey ends here."

The screen showed Jane, looking as beautiful as ever, but Lizzy could tell she was shocked. She squeezed Jane's hand as she watched Jane, on screen, walking across the floor to meet Charles. Her breath caught. Had they somehow fixed it? Did Jane and Charles end up together? How could Jane have kept this from her?

Her hopes were dashed by the small smile that Charles pulled. A reality dating show had never hurt so hard. He looked truly remorseful.

"Jane. You are. So wonderful. Thank you for coming on this journey with me." The words weren't his; pumped, no doubt, into his ear, by William. At that moment she almost hated him. How could he keep them apart?

Jane smiled sweetly and blinked rapidly, but a single tear escaped and slid down her cheek. A sniff came from the real Jane sitting next to her and Lizzy felt a hole open in her chest.

"Charles." Her smile faltered then resurfaced. "Thank you. I can't tell you what this has meant to me." She kissed him on the cheek and the camera followed her solitary figure across the room.

It was so quiet, Lizzy was sure the others could hear her heart beating against her ribs.

Bill Lucas appeared again, his cheer was forced. "The lucky couple will..."

Where was her exit? What happened?

Bill finished his spiel and was replaced with an image of Lizzy smiling. She was wearing the same dress so it must have been from earlier that evening.

Her mouth dropped open. They weren't going to show it.

Tinkly music started playing and the image segued to show them standing under the blossoms. Lizzy smiled at Charles, went up on her toes to put her arms around his neck. She could almost hear William's voice urging Charles to kiss her, feel Charles' arms around her waist, his body pressed against hers. And there it was. The kiss. The camera had caught her mouth curving into a smile against his lips. They separated and it looked like they were gazing into each other's eyes, completely unaware of the world around them. Then – credits.

"What the hell was that?" burst out of Lizzy before she realised what she was saying.

All eyes were on her. Kitty spoke first, a note of reverence in her voice. "Lizzy, you won."

"But I–but I didn't," she protested. Jane squeezed her hand and she started to come back into her body. "Did you know they were going to do this?"

Jane shook her head. "I didn't know what they were going to do."

"What's wrong?" Charlotte asked.

Lizzy shook off Jane's hand and held up one finger. "I need to make a phone call. Give me a second please. I don't want to waste this anger."

Everyone looked alarmed – Kitty and Mary looked at each other then at Lizzy, Jane opened her mouth and reached out but Lizzy jumped up. No one tried to stop her.

The feeling of unreality was familiar but there were no cameras this time. The short walk to her bedroom looked the same but somehow everything was different. This was his fault. He'd done ...*something.*

William was the top name in her recent call list, this call was going to be different from their last, no cute banter this time.

She paced her bedroom waiting for him to answer.

"Hi, Lizzy. How lovely to hear from you."

"Cut the crap, William. I saw the show tonight."

"You–you didn't like it?"

"Are you kidding? It was terrible! That was a pathetic ending and you know it! Plus it wasn't what *actually* happened."

His sigh came down the phone line. "Nothing in TV is ever what actually happened. None of it is real. You know that. You told me that."

"It doesn't seem fair to–to lie to the audience like that. Make them think it was a happy ending when it was a disaster."

"Everyone wants a happy ending. What would you rather I did – throw you under the bus? I wouldn't do that to you. The sponsors wanted a nice conclusion, I had to appease them. I thought maybe you'd be relieved. No one needs to know what really happened."

"Because I came off so badly you mean?" she accused, waving her free arm wildly.

"Lizzy, that's not fair. I understand where you were coming from. Sure, I didn't get it at the time, but I do now. Not everyone would understand. They could be angry with you."

“Stop saying rational things.” She stamped her feet. “I want to be angry with you!”

“I’m sorry?”

She took a deep breath and released it slowly. *Be reasonable, don’t blow this*. “I have to go. I have guests.” *I can’t breakdown till they’re gone.*

“Are we–are we ok?”

“I don’t know.” She pulled the phone away, ready to disconnect without saying goodbye but reconsidered. “Me yelling at you is kind of our thing.” God, she sounded like a teenager. “I’m sure we’ll be fine. Bye.”

She dropped onto the bed with a sigh, rubbed her forehead and tapped her phone screen. She sent William a thumbs up emoji and a kissing face.

She shook her shoulders, trying to remove some of the heaviness of that conversation. She tidied the bed coverings before returning to the lounge.

“Who were you yelling at?” Kitty asked immediately, she’s moved to the side of Mary’s chair facing the bedroom door and looked ready to pounce.

“We tried not to listen,” Charlotte put in apologetically, she was sitting on the couch with her arm around Jane.

“Are you ok?” Jane asked, she looked like she’d been crying.

Mary said nothing, she simply looked disappointed. She’d been looking forward to seeing a woman reject the boyfriend. This ending wasn’t the empowering or dramatic one they’d discussed over their first dinner.

“More wine?” Lizzy offered. They erupted in questions like she’d popped champagne. She raised her hands in defence. “I’m not blowing you off, I’ll tell you everything. I just need… fortification.” And tomorrow she’d work on cutting down her intake.

Post Broadcast

"Wow, I did not expect that," Charlotte said, when Lizzy had finished her story.

"I knew some of that," Mary said.

"Me too," Jane said, "I was there, at least for the first bit."

They turned to Kitty who was, essentially, the outsider in the group. She didn't say anything.

Lizzy stopped pacing and sat in the chair Charlotte usually occupied.

"I'm not sure," Lizzy said, "how much of that I'm allowed to have told anyone. What with the NDA and everything. The stuff about my personal life is, well, personal, so I guess that's my decision but it's also about William's life so to a certain extent it's up to him too and now I don't know if I should have said anything at all, except you heard me yelling at him, and I wasn't exactly going to kick you out without any explanation—" Her speech became more and more rapid as she went on, until Jane put a hand on her arm.

"We're your friends. We aren't going to share your secrets, right?" She glanced around at the group; everyone nodded.

Kitty finally spoke. "While I appreciate you wanting the truth to be portrayed, it would interrupt the heavily manicured narrative of the format." Lizzy frowned at Mary's words coming from Kitty's mouth. "Not to mention it would piss off the advertisers." That sounded more like Kitty. "Did they even pay for anything?"

Lizzy shrugged. "We don't exactly talk about finances. But yeah, that's pretty much what he said too – gotta keep the money people happy."

Mary chimed in with, "I don't like saying this, but I agree with Caroline." Even Jane gasped. "She brought up the fact that we didn't have confessionals. Obviously they couldn't sponsor any one-on-one time with the women and the camera or any behind the scenes, emotional stuff, even fights. But that's the stuff that really sells the format." She shifted in her chair onto her knees. "Hear me out. How great would Caroline be? With Charles she's lovely but behind the scenes she's picking fights and bullying the crew. There's a whole layer the audience misses and she gets to become the true villain we know she is." She flung an arm towards the couch. "Jane cries to the camera about her feelings for Charles and even though it's not evident in their dates the viewer can connect with that and root for her to win and be devastated when she doesn't. It pulls on the heart strings and pulls us into the show."

"Um," Jane said.

"Yeah, sorry for using you as an example. But knowing how you feel about Charles made watching this so much more impactful for me."

Jane cleared her throat. "I don't ah...."

"I've gotta admit, behind the scenes are my favourite part," Kitty agreed.

"Mine too," Charlotte said. "Not that I watch a lot of this, or anything."

"Sure, sure," Mary said, "you just agreed to be on one."

Charlotte reached across to lightly smack Mary on the shoulder. "That was promotion for my business."

"I hate to break up the party but I have work in the morning," Jane said. Phones were pulled out and the time marvelled at and faster than Lizzy could have imagined, she was alone again.

She sat on the couch, considered tidying up the scattered wine glasses and empty snack bowls but instead pushed them aside, to plant her feet on the coffee table which lurched at the weight, causing a wine glass to slip off the edge. It landed on the carpet so remained intact. With a swear word Lizzy swiped it up before the tiny remainder of pink wine could seep out. Grumbling she collected the debris and put them on the bench in the kitchen.

When she checked her phone there was a text from Gina that she ignored. Instead she spent another half an hour scrolling through pictures, eventually purchasing a replacement coffee table before dragging herself into bed.

The expected breakdown never came. Maybe there was something in talking things out.

**

MUM: *The shop was overrun with people this weekend after the show!*

LIZZY: *Wasn't that the point?*

MUM: *Don't sass me, young lady. You nearly ruined my business*

Lizzy refused to apologise for her decision so she tapped her phone screen off and got out of bed.

She slid into her desk half an hour later, noticing that although she was later than normal she was still earlier than some of the designers. Mondays were a slow start but hopefully that meant she could get some work done in peace.

Denny poked his head out of his office, "Lizzy."

She tensed as he walked over, expecting a reprimand she tried to push her bag under the desk with her foot.

"If your mother hadn't got in first we could have used the publicity from the show. Done their graphics – whoever they had was shit." He saluted her with his coffee cup.

"Um, thanks?"

"My wife loved the show. Forbade me to talk to you about it till it was done so I wouldn't get any spoilers."

"I–I'm not allowed to talk about the show anyway?" Why was everything she said coming out like a question?

"How was the trip?"

"What trip? Oh – *oh*, right the trip that Charles and I 'won' from the show! We haven't actually done that. Yet. I don't know if – yeah." She worried she may have said too much but Denny didn't react.

"You let me know when you need the leave and I'll approve it."

"It's only a couple of nights. We could go in the weekend." She was frowning, she could feel her face frowning; that was not the appropriate way to look when talking about going on holiday with your boyfriend. She shot a panicked look at Kitty who was passing on her way to the kitchen then smoothed her brow with effort and pulled a smile. "Thank you, I'll keep that in mind."

"Lizzy!" Kitty had heard her silent plea. "I need to talk to you about that thing, sorry to interrupt, Denny."

"No, no; we were done," and he took himself back to his office.

"That looked awkward."

"Thanks for saving me." She slumped back against her chair. "He was trying to talk about the show. I mean, he *was* talking about the show. I just don't know what to say to people."

Kitty tapped her fingers on the desk. "You don't *have* to say anything. I imagine the show will release a statement stating that sadly, you and Charles are no longer together."

Lizzy pressed her lips together, her eyes on Kitty's still tapping fingers.

"Or, you know, you could talk to your boyfriend, ask him what the show is going to do." She was grinning when Lizzy looked up to glare at her. "Just a suggestion." She chuckled as she walked back to her desk.

KITTY: *I don't know what to do with myself now the show is over. I'll miss you guys*

JANE: *We'll still see each other!*

LIZZY: *I mean, you're not getting rid of me that easily Kitty*

LIZZY: *Also, we work together*

MARY: *You know what we should do? We should stage our own reunion*

MARY: *Without cameras*

JANE: *It might help diffuse some tension*

KITTY: *Can I come?*

MARY: *I say yes but it should be a consensus. We should invite the others too*

JANE: *Is anyone in contact with Lydia or Caroline?*

CHARLOTTE: *I bet Lizzy could get everyone's details from that guy she yelled at*

LIZZY: *Traitor*

After Party

A week later Lizzy was adjusting her dress in the barn/event venue at Pemberley vineyards that was somehow both rustic and chic. Attending parties here was becoming a habit. Watch parties didn't count as parties, right? She might need to get out more.

"You know you really didn't have to do this," she said, half wishing she hadn't agreed to it herself.

William smiled down at her. "I want to meet your friends. As your friends. Not as contestants."

"Without your discount I doubt we could have afforded this. Did I thank you for that? I meant to thank you."

"You can thank me latter."

She grinned at his implication. "It's a huge room for so few of us." It would be impossible to avoid anyone.

"I'm sorry more of the crew couldn't come. It was kind of you to think of them." He wiped his hand down his jawline. "They *did* have a wrap party...and, ah, we didn't invite *any* of the contestants to that." He took a gulp of wine and looked away guiltily. "In my defence, I didn't organise it. Maybe they wanted space to be able to..."

"Bitch about us?" she offered with a tight smile.

"I'm not the one that said that."

Gina's arrival saved him.

"Everything is in order. Food will come out at half-hour intervals. Fresh wine will circulate every fifteen minutes." She bounced a little; it was a huge contrast to the last party Lizzy had seen her at. "I'm so excited to meet everyone. Is Jane as beautiful in person?"

William said, "What?" at the same time Lizzy was assuring her that Jane was indeed as beautiful in real life as she was on screen.

"You were watching?" he demanded, half authoritarian, half concerned, all protective older brother.

Gina shrugged. "I'm ok. My therapist said it was ok, it might even be good for me, but to keep checking in with myself. I loved it. I wish my season had ended differently but I can't change that. Plus, I get the super-secret behind-the-scenes scoop because I knew the *real* love story that was going on." She grinned and jostled her brother with her shoulder.

Love wasn't a word they'd uttered yet – it was far too soon. They were still working out the bounds of their relationship. They looked at each other awkwardly, stiffened then avoided eye contact.

"Guys, this is your first public engagement," – Lizzy winced at Gina's choice of words – "people are going to have questions and make assumptions." They heard a car pull up outside. "I'll go greet them while you sort yourselves out." With a look at her bother she turned and hurried out.

William cleared his throat. "Why do I feel like I'm back in high school again?" He pulled his suit jacket tighter.

"Because your sister is calling you out?" Lizzy straightened her shoulders, bracing herself. "That could be my mother in that car—"

"*You invited your mother?*"

"Did I forget to mention that? Wow, we really do need to work on communication." Muffled voices came nearer. "Ok, quick. Um, do you want to be boyfriend/girlfriend – with previously discussed stipulations of non-exclusivity? Yes, I researched terms," she said, accurately judging the look on his face.

"Um, yep."

"Good."

"Good." A smile broke over William's face. "Girlfriend," he said and offered his glass. She tapped it with hers, "Boyfriend."

"Further discussion to follow later," Lizzy said hurriedly, but she wasn't sure William heard her over—

"I am ready to get *lit* tonight!" It was Lydia, resplendent in sparkly eyeshadow, with an audacious feather boa around her shoulders and an apologetic Kitty on her arm. They trotted up and Lydia batted her eyelash extensions at William. "Hello producer man, this is my *girlfriend*, Kitty. I'm a *lesbian* now."

Lizzy raised her eyebrows at Kitty, who shrugged and murmured, "We talked about your partner not defining your sexuality, I guess it didn't stick." She was pulled into an introduction with William, who reached out to put an arm around Lizzy.

"I'm sure you remember my *girlfriend*," he put the tiniest emphasis on the word; perhaps to mimic Lydia, perhaps because he was proud they'd just defined that.

Lydia enveloped Lizzy in an alcohol-scented hug, somehow managing to bring Kitty along. Kitty patted Lizzy's shoulder and reminded Lydia they worked together when she attempted to introduce them.

Lizzy conducted a silent conversation with Kitty about Lydia's state; a drinking gesture was performed and "pre-loaded" was mouthed. It looked like Kitty would have to trade her evening of fan-girling for girlfriending.

"Food will come around every half hour," Lizzy directed this at Kitty, who gave her an appreciative nod before she was dragged off by Lydia in pursuit of a drink. "Oh wow, just, wow," she murmured as they walked away.

"The drinking or the *lesbian*?" William mimicked Lydia's delivery.

"Maybe both," Lizzy muttered out the side of her mouth before they were distracted by the next arrivals; there would be time for a thorough debrief later.

**

"Charles *is* coming, right?" Mary asked.

Charlotte looked over at Jane, who was chatting with a remarkably comfortable Gina; maybe Jane's lovely personality had won out over Gina's introversion. "I hope for Jane's sake he does. That is why you organised this, right?"

Lizzy held up her hands. "This whole party wasn't my idea. I have the receipts." Hadn't Mary suggested it first? She had only stepped in when venues were being discussed, to suggest the vineyard as a better option than her living room.

"But you didn't have to capitulate," Mary explained. "You got your boyfriend to offer this place, organise the food and the wine, invite everyone..."

"To be fair, Gina did most of that. Apart from the inviting, because privacy. Turns out she loved the show."

"She's sweet," Mary said thoughtfully. "And, looks like I'm single since Kitty's taken." She jerked her head over to the corner where Lydia and Kitty were making out. "Do they *have* to? How did they even meet?"

Lizzy shrugged. "I'm as surprised as you are. Kitty said she was seeing someone, but I didn't know it was Lydia. If I'd known you were into her I would have warned you."

"I think Jane might be the only straight one among us. I know, I know – Caroline," Charlotte said over their objections. "But I'm not sure if there's a sexuality for someone who only cares about themselves, and will sleep with anyone if it serves them. I'm reasonably sure she'd still be draped all over Bill if his name was Bil-linda. You know, like Belinda."

The grimaced at the lame joke and Charlotte asked Lizzy how things were at work. She and Mary were both interested in Lizzy's idea to engage a representative from the local iwi as a cultural advisor, something that had been percolating in the back of her mind since they hired Kitty.

**

Predictably, her mother made an Entrance. Unpredictably, that entrance was on the arm of Charles.

"Mum?" Lizzy rushed over, noticing how Charles was supporting rather than leading her, she looked pale and frazzled.

"Lizzy, isn't he a knight in shining armour?" her mother gushed, leaning into her hero, her voice soft. "Charles is such a good boy." She patted his arm while Charles blushed. "Isn't my Lizzy lovely, Charles dear? Why don't the two of you catch up?"

"Let's get you a seat first," Charles suggested and led her towards an empty table.

"Not much of a party, is it?" her mother murmured, looking around.

"Sadly, most of the crew were tied up on other jobs and unable to make it," William came out of nowhere, a comforting presence at Lizzy's side. "Are you all right? Do you need anything?"

Her mother's eyes narrowed, and Lizzy intervened before she started treating William like her personal servant.

"Mum, this is William, my boyfriend and our host – this is his vineyard. He's also an old friend of Charles'," she added hastily. "William, this is my mother, Eliza."

William offered his hand, which she shook. "It's a pleasure to see you again," he said. "Now, is there anything I can get you?"

She waved her hands in a pushing gesture. "Stop hovering, go get me a drink, I've had a nasty shock. No, not you, Lizzy," her voice suddenly sharp. "I'd like to talk with you, young lady."

Charles gave her a sympathetic smile; William raised his eyebrows, asking if she wanted him to stay. She shook her head. She could handle her mother.

"That was rude," she said as she sat down. "They were only trying to be nice. What happened to you?"

Her mother frowned. "Rude is introducing me to your boyfriend with no warning after I went to all the trouble of getting Charles buttered up for you." Once the scrutiny had disappeared she held herself differently; her posture was straight, her gaze direct. She was no longer the weak older lady and Lizzy suspected she'd been playing a part.

"Mum, what did you do?"

"Nothing, nothing. Oh well, all right. I may have called Charles to play the knight in shining armour to a helpless lady with car troubles, then extolled your virtues in the ride over here. I got him to offer to drive you home too, in the hopes that you'd come to your senses and he could kiss you at the door."

Lizzy put her head in her hands. "Mum, you need to stop—"

William arrived with juice but was berated for not bringing alcohol.

"Can't you see I've had a hard night?"

He went away again.

"All my work for nothing," she muttered. "You ungrateful child."

Lizzy, accustomed to her mother's outbursts, didn't take this to heart. She knew once her mother had a few drinks in her things would look different.

"How did you contact Charles?"

"I have my ways. I'm very resourceful."

William returned with a glass of wine, "from our own vintage." Her mother looked at him, assessing, and he backed away.

"Did you say he owns this vineyard?"

She replied that she believed he shared ownership with his sister.

"Not too shabby." She sipped the wine. "Hmm, not too shabby. Maybe you're not a complete waste after all, my girl."

"Thanks Mum." She took a deep breath – in for a penny, in for a pound. "He's one of the producers from the show. *The* producer. The whole production was his baby. He's quite successful, travels for work but this is his home base."

"He's quite handsome, a bit stuck up at first but ever so nice about my fudge. Does he want kids?"

"We've never—"

"Perhaps you might forget to take your contraception and—"

"I'm going to pretend I didn't hear that." Lizzy scanned the guests, desperate for an excuse to change the conversation.

Jane was edging around the room. Surreptitiously playing keep away from Charles, she managed to be at a different table every time he reached where she had been. Hadn't Lizzy just thought it would be impossible to avoid each other in a room this large? Jane seemed set to prove her wrong.

She waved her over and Jane took a seat on the other side of her mother. Lizzy introduced them with a smile.

"Aren't you lovely, why would a girl like you have to go on a dating show?"

Lizzy closed her eyes in pain and embarrassment.

"You know, I thought the same thing when I met Lizzy. Why hasn't she been snapped up yet? But, you know, we live in a small and unvarying community. People are born here, live here, die here. It's one of the things I love about this place, but it means you don't often meet new people."

"Funny then that none of us knew each other beforehand," Lizzy intervened before her mother could say anything else. "My mother runs the craft shop in town."

"Oh I knew you looked familiar," Jane said. "Charles and I..." she faltered for a moment, blinking, then rallied. "Charles and I had a date at your store, it's quite charming. One of my aunts is a regular there."

Praising her mother's store was a good way to go, although detailed questioning followed until her mother had discovered exactly who Jane's aunt was. Lizzy felt she could leave them to it; her mother flapped her hand to send her away when she asked if they'd be ok without her. With a sigh of relief Lizzy escaped.

She apologised to William as soon as she reached him. He opened his mouth, then closed it. He cleared his throat.

"I wanted to say I can see where you get it from...then realised how offensive that would sound."

"Yet, you still said it."

"Maybe I should stop talking altogether?"

She smiled at him and put her arm through his, turning to survey the room.

"It really is a pathetic turn out. But somehow Jane is still managing to avoid Charles."

"You noticed that too."

"I didn't get the chance to say hello properly to him when he arrived, I was too focused on Mum. Does he know about us?"

William led her over to where Charles was talking to Mary, muttering quickly, "we haven't spoken much since the final." Lizzy turned to him with a look of surprise but there wasn't time to ask questions.

Lizzy took the lead. "Charles, good to see you." She put a hand on him arm. "Of course, you know my boyfriend, William."

Charles eyebrows rose in surprise. "Boyfriend? I don't think anyone has ever used that term about William in the whole time I've known him. How did you manage to snag him?"

Mary snorted, then immediately pretended she hadn't.

"My stunning charm of course – I can't compete with Jane on looks." She followed Charles' glance to where Jane was still talking with her mother; Charlotte had joined them.

"She yelled at me," William blurted, and all attention turned to him. "Well, you did. Several times in fact."

Mary snorted again and murmured "enemies to lovers" into her wine glass.

"How is your dissertation going, Mary?" Lizzy turned the conversation on her. "Can we call you Dr Mary yet?"

"Doctor? Are you a doctor?" Charles asked. "You were always terribly smart, too smart for me."

Lizzy suppressed a groan and gave Mary a look which clearly said "don't." Mary opened her mouth but Charles was saved by Lydia's appearance.

"Charlie-boy!" Lydia hurled herself into Charles' arms, sending his wine flying. Gina rushed over to clean up the mess while Lydia introduced Kitty, who had trailed behind her.

"Kitty and I are colleagues—" Lizzy said, but Lydia interrupted "—she's *my* girlfriend."

Charles blinked and Lizzy wondered if he wished there was a little voice in his ear telling him how to handle this situation. Next to her William tensed like he wanted to slide back into that role. After a pause Charles extended his hand to Kitty and asked how they had met.

With Lydia dominating the conversation, Mary drifted away and William tugged on Lizzy's arm. She allowed him to lead her towards a fresh glass of wine.

He glanced between the two main groups – the gathering around her mother and the gathering around Charles – and noticed Bill Lucas and Caroline, ensconced in a corner, intent on each other.

"I'm going to have to intervene," he said with a sigh. "This isn't going to plan."

"Intervene? What plan? William, what have you been concocting? If we're a couple we should really be scheming together."

He rubbed the back of his neck. "I'd hoped that getting them in the same room would be enough, and when so few people RSVP'd I thought it would be inevitable. But even with this pathetic turn out," he gestured at the mostly empty room, "they're still managing to avoid each other."

"Charles and Jane."

He nodded.

"Technically she's avoiding him. That was my plan too, just kinda...leave them to it. But now they're managing to pretend they don't notice the other person is there. This is such a waste. What can we do?"

"Well...if this was the show I'd force them into close quarters and ply them with alcohol. Maybe we should have moved to a smaller location..."

“Nothing to say we still can’t,” Lizzy declared, and she headed for Gina who froze like a deer in headlights, seeming more like her usual self than she had all night. “Nothing’s wrong, you’re doing a great job,” Lizzy assured Gina. “I was just thinking you might have a more intimate setting we could all retire to? Perhaps we could have the canapes served on plates in the dining room up at the house then we could—”

“Go in the lounge and open the big doors onto the balcony to create more space. It might be a little cramped but it’s got to be better than this. I wish I’d thought of it earlier.” Gina hurried away.

William caught up to Lizzy, “What was that about?” he asked, as he watched his sister’s departing back.

“Change of location is required. Gina’s going to move us up to the house instead. They can try to avoid each other there.”

“I’ve never seen her like this,” William said, a note of wonder in his voice. “She’s so...capable. I’ve been thinking we could use an event planner – she’d be perfect.”

By the simple expedient of Lizzy asking Jane to sit next to her and William asking Charles to sit next to him they finally managed to get the reluctant couple within speaking distance. Gina had made it appear the move had always been the plan with a simple “dessert will be served in the house.” Perhaps, like her brother, she found confidence – and performed better – in situations where she knew her role and had some level of control.

William leant toward Lizzy from his seat at the head of the table and murmured that he’d managed a quick talk with Charles on the way over.

"You tell me that now?" she hissed, wishing she'd taken the opportunity to speak with Jane.

"So, Jane," she said brightly, turning to her, "how are your kids?" Out of the corner of her eye she noticed Charles shift. "Did I tell you, William, that Jane works in early childhood?" She managed to include Charles in this comment. All three turned to look at Jane, who suddenly looked self-conscious.

"Well," she said to her plate, where she pushed around a delicacy with her fork, "the kids are always growing, developing, learning new things. They have a resiliency that..." Her voice faltered but she cleared her throat and looked up. "We can learn a lot from children. They are often overlooked and not taken seriously."

Lizzy winced, hoping this wasn't levelled at Charles, but Jane's face was clear and there was no malice in her voice.

"I remember you telling me how hard it was to leave them – even for a week," Charles offered. His voice faltered as Jane turned her gaze on him, but he smiled at her. "I remember thinking how–how important your work was to you and I wanted to feel that passionate about...anything."

William leaned back in his chair, looking out the door, "Lizzy, it looks like Gina needs us. Charles, can you keep Jane company till we get back?" He stood and offered Charles his chair which was taken with alacrity.

That was a bit heavy-handed but Lizzy rose also, pulling a face at William. He glared at her chair until she turned back with a sigh. "Jane, would you...?"

Jane looked up at her, then over at Charles who was busily swapping plates, then back at Lizzy again, lost. Lizzy nodded encouragingly and

Jane's obliging nature won out as she moved chairs. Lizzy pushed down a twinge of guilt, she was only helping Jane do something she already wanted to do.

William walked past the kitchen and into the entrance, surprising Lizzy by sweeping her into his arms. She squeaked.

"You almost ruined that for us, Mister."

"I think I salvaged it in the end," he said and leant down to kiss her.

Lizzy allowed herself to be carried away by his touch till a sound alerted her that they weren't alone and she jerked back.

"Don't mind me," Charlotte said, with a grin on her face, when Lizzy spotted her. "I was heading for the bathroom, they said it was down here."

"How are things in there?" Lizzy asked, tilting her head back towards the dining room.

"Caroline took a phone call and I think Bill is flirting with your mother." Lizzy made an involuntary movement forward but stopped herself at the look on Charlotte's face, she did not want to interfere in her mother's life. "But you mean the golden couple, don't you? They're fine, they've got a little space from everyone else, heads together, talking. I think it's finally working, so long as you two stay out here." She pointed at the floor. "Now, if you'll excuse me?"

William looked caught out like a guilty schoolkid; he avoided eye contact with Charlotte and merely nodded. Lizzy laughed at him quietly and suggested they siphon guests off into the lounge. With some clever manoeuvring, all that were left in the dining room were "the golden couple" at one end of the table and Lizzy's mum with Bill at the other. Caroline was nowhere to be found.

"You don't suppose she's rifling through my underwear drawer?" William asked.

"Is that where you keep your valuables?"

Most of the waiters had left and Gina was serving coffee. Lydia, the one who perhaps needed it the most, was the only one who refused. She was currently dancing to music no one else could hear, under the night sky on the balcony, while Kitty hovered in the doorway.

Caroline appeared out of the night, narrowly avoiding a collision with Lydia who then tried to drag her into an embrace. She shook off Lydia, adjusted her dress and re-entered the house, glanced around the living room dismissing them all with a shrug. Gina offered her coffee as she headed for the door, but she refused rudely. When Lizzy came to Gina's defence Caroline called them both "coffee girls", collected her coat and was gone again.

"That was unpleasant," Mary said coming up to pat Gina's shoulder. "You did a great job."

Charlotte and Mary left together with a "good luck" and a glance towards the dining room.

"Have your mother call me," Charlotte said. "I've been trying to contact her for weeks. I didn't want to talk shop tonight." She hesitated a moment. "And if you want to talk more about work, call me."

"Do you want to have lunch?"

"Sorry, I'm busy," Lizzy said with a brief glance at Kitty.

After a moment Lizzy realised that Kitty had stepped away, then come back. She turned to look at her.

"Are you mad at me for dating Lydia, or not telling you I'm dating Lydia?" Her voice was high and several of the guys turned from their desks to look.

Lizzy blinked. "No, I'm in the middle of invoicing and I have lunch plans with Jane." She held up one finger, saved her work and gestured for Kitty to follow her to the kitchen.

They leaned against opposite cabinets; Lizzy wanted to step forward to hug Kitty but her arms were folded across her chest, practically screaming 'do not touch me'.

"You barely talked to me at the party. You haven't said a word to me all day."

"It looked like you had your hands full at the party—" Lizzy stopped as Kitty tensed further, she reassessed. "I'm sorry. You're right, I have been glued to my screen and ignoring everyone today, including you. And maybe I was a little blindsided seeing you with Lydia. You told me you were seeing someone but you didn't say who. And maybe, yeah, I was a little...jealous. That's on me. I'm sorry." When Kitty finally looked at her she turned her gaze to the floor. "We're friends and you deserved better than that."

Kitty smacked her lips. "A part of me didn't *want* to tell you, to tell all the girls, that I was dating Lydia. We made so much fun of her at the viewing parties. And she's kind of a mess," Kitty snorted a laugh that shifted into a wry smile, "but she's also great and so much fun."

Lizzy shrugged. “You like who you like.” She glanced out the kitchen door. “I don’t tend to live my personal life at work,” she explained, turning back, “partly because until recently I didn’t *have* a personal life. But that’s a whole other thing.” She ran her hands through her hair, having a life outside of work was not sustainable with her workload. “I do have lunch plans though. Do you want to maybe get a drink after work or have lunch tomorrow instead?”

Kitty nodded, her body language softening as she released her folded arms. Maybe the reason Lizzy hadn’t had friends before wasn’t because they’d all moved away, but because she just wasn’t very good at keeping them. She reached for Kitty’s arm, a soft touch.

“I’m sorry. I promise I’ll be better, or at least I’ll try. Just, you know, call me out.”

Kitty smiled at her and the tension inside Lizzy’s chest eased.

**

“Am I a good friend?” she asked Jane at lunch.

“Lizzy, you’re a lovely friend. I’m glad you’re my friend,” Jane said sincerely.

“Kitty accused me of being pissed at her for keeping Lydia from us, and maybe I was a little. But *I* did the same thing. None of you knew I was dating William till after the finale.”

Jane pursed her lips. “With the production...you wouldn’t want anyone to know...right?”

“Well, yeah. But I couldn’t confide in my friends?” She shook her head to clear the thoughts. “I don’t know, I’m being weird, ignore me. I wanted to ask how you were after the party?" It was the entire motivation for this lunch.

"Oh, I was fine. No hangover, I was pretty careful. I've been drinking so much more than I usually do with our girls' nights."

"Tell me about it. I'm almost glad William goes away for work, I drink so much when he's around. Oh, wow, that sounds bad, I mean he *does* own a vineyard. But anyway, that wasn't what I meant." She took a deep breath and chose her words carefully, "How did you feel about seeing Charles again?"

"It was a good party. I hope that we'll keep in contact even though the show is over," Jane said avoiding eye contact and sipping her drink.

Lizzy couldn't help but smile.

"Stop it, Lizzy." She set her drink down. "I understand him better now, he's...nice...charming...he was...going along with the show. It didn't mean anything."

Lizzy nodded, smirking. "Nice. Charming," she echoed.

"It was a fleeting thing."

"Fleeting, right." Lizzy didn't believe her.

"I'm not–I'm not saying the show wasn't a positive experience. I met you." She smiled fondly at Lizzy and touched her hand. "I learnt a lot about myself. I grew. I–I started therapy again. I don't think I'm the same person I was before the show, during the show."

Gina had said something similar; she was in therapy too.

"Maybe I should start therapy," Lizzy mused aloud. "Work on my Daddy issues." *And my underlying questions about my sexuality. And why I didn't have friends. And why I over commit myself at work.* "And...other stuff." She wasn't who she'd been at the start of filming either.

The waitress delivered their meals; Lizzy noticed that for the first time that Jane dove straight in.

**

LIZZY: *It didn't work. I can't believe it didn't work*

WILLIAM: *Jane and Charles you mean?*

LIZZY: *All that work, wasted. What do we do now?*

WILLIAM: *You can't push people into love*

WILLIAM: *Yes, I am aware that is literally my job. Sometimes*

LIZZY: *What do we do? How do we fix this?*

WILLIAM: *I don't know if we can*

Lizzy threw her phone down in disgust. She wanted to argue that he should be supporting her but it didn't seem like he wasn't. She reached down and picked her phone up again.

LIZZY: *I feel like a failure*

If she was being honest it felt like she was failing in every aspect of life. Not only had she failed to reunite Jane and Charles but things at work hadn't been great either. When she wasn't working crazy hours she couldn't handle the workload and Denny had rejected her idea for hiring a cultural advisor.

WILLIAM: *Anything I say can't change the way you feel*

She rolled her eyes.

WILLIAM: *I don't think you're a failure*

She smiled; for now that would have to do.

Happy Endings

"I don't know how to get them together. Jane seems have to given up!" Lizzy dropped back on the pillows in frustration.

William smiled down at her as he threw a pair of socks into the open suitcase at the bottom of the bed.

"What's the prayer that the alcoholics say? God, grant me the serenity..." he ducked the pillow Lizzy threw at him and laughed.

"It's admirable that you want your friends to be happy, but you need to, um, admit...realise...? understand...? understand that they are in control of their actions. Just as *you* are in charge of *yours*. Which includes not throwing another pillow at me. Don't think I don't see what you're doing."

Lizzy sighed and released the pillow.

"Jane's too stuck in traditional gender roles to ever make a move – and she's got a fear of rejection too. Charles is such a spineless twit he won't make a move unless you tell him to..."

"Hey! That is my friend you're calling a spineless twit!" He turned from the wardrobe, hands on his hips, ready to fight, but there was laughter in his voice. He was building up a head of steam for one of their classic arguments but Lizzy forestalled him.

In a slowing, marvelling voice she repeated, "...unless you tell him to... That's it!" She lurched into a sitting position. "William, you have to call Charles! You have to tell him–tell him to–to kiss Jane! No, that's too much. To ask Jane out." She swung her head wildly from side to side. "Where's your cell phone?"

"In my pocket. But honey, I can't. I've sworn off meddling." His hands dropped to his sides. "They're adults. They have free will. If they like each other, they'll figure it out."

"No, but I—" she was almost crying in frustration. This was the last time she'd see him for a month and she was ruining it. She should be focusing on him instead.

William perched on the edge of the bed next to her, putting his hand on her leg.

"I know. I want to make everything right too. I got him into this mess. Both of them. You really think Jane is genuinely interested in Charles? No–no, I'm not doubting," he said quickly as she began to bristle. "Charles is into her. We give them space to sort it out themselves. That's all we can do."

He leaned forward and kissed her. "I like that you want what's best for people. And I like the sound that you make when I kiss you here..." his mouth moved to her neck. She giggled and fell back on the bed, William on top of her.

Something he'd said stuck in her mind – "you only want what's best for people". That sounded suspiciously like what her mother always said when she attempted to force Lizzy into a date – or a dating show – "I only want what's best for you." Adding that to her mental list of things to discuss at therapy, she pushed her mother out of her mind so she could focus on the delicious sensations William was provoking.

She'd found her happy ending. She wasn't going to manufacture one for Jane and Charles; they could find their own.

Outro

KITTY: *Look what I found! We can discuss at girls' night, I'll remind Gina it's her turn to host*

(Screenshot with annotations)

> It's been a year since *Bag a Boyfriend*, the local reality show that became a cult classic thanks to the internet, graced our screens. Images of the show have been turned into GIFs and memes, now used by people who have no idea of their origin. *What did we do before the internet??* We decided to check in on the cast to find out where they are now.
>
> Mary, the first contestant to leave the show, has also left town. She earned her doctorate in literature and now teaches at Lincoln University. *Yes Dr Mary!*
>
> Charlotte is a prominent voice in the local business community. Her accounting firm specialises in fostering women-owned and new businesses.
>
> Lydia announced her engagement to a woman online last year but seems to have finished experimenting – her social feed now has photos of her with a man. *Bi-erasure.*
>
> Caroline had a brief stint as a local spokesperson but after rumours surfaced that she was difficult to work with she cut her contracts and can now be seen as background talent on our nation's favourite soap *Shortland Street.*

Like Caroline, Jane's face has been seen all over town promoting local businesses. Unlike Caroline, she remains as approachable and down to earth as she ever was.

Lizzy, the "winner" of the season, is dating one of the producers from the show in a long-distance relationship and working alongside Charlotte as her business manager.

In the grand tradition of reality TV couples, Charles and Lizzy appear to have broken up by the time of screening. But in an interesting twist Charles has been seen about town with the runner up, Jane. There appears to be no animosity as the couple have been spotted double dating with Lizzy and her man.

There are rumours of a second season, with Charles, following in the footsteps of Bachelor Art Green, coming on board as host. *Is this true??*

LIZZY: *I'm sure William would have mentioned it. Unless he wasn't allowed to because of his contract*

JANE: *I'm asking Charles right now*

CHARLOTTE: *Do you suppose they'll need someone to manage the finances?*

MARY: *If it's true I demand virtual screenings #charliesangels*

LIZZY: *#friendsforlife*

Acknowledgements

In January 2022 I attended a virtual book club meeting of the Hawai'i branch of the Jane Austen Society of North America, we were discussing a modern novel based off one of Austen's classics. The attendees were appalled that the author didn't credit Jane Austen in her acknowledgements while I guiltily attempted to recall if I'd ever mentioned her in my own, despite all my books being derivative of her work. With that in mind my first acknowledgement is Jane Austen. Without her writing I would be a different person, this book would not exist, none of my books would exist, I might not be a writer and would never have met some of my dearest friends. I wish I had a fraction of her talent and dedication, her resoluteness in a society that didn't her value her brain (or indeed her body for anything other than childbearing).

Reality TV is a guilty pleasure for me. The shows I feel the most drawn to are those that delve into human relationships and love – *The Bachelor*, *The Bachelorette* and *Married at First Sight*. I eagerly watched the few local seasons of these shows, each with a slant that made them more relevant than the international versions. I wasn't into the drama, I didn't want to see cat fights or highly choreographed arguments; I wanted to see the human connection. As drama took over more and more of the reality TV formats, the truth was left behind and people were being used like puppets, their emotions left in the dust. I wanted to explore this a little on a smaller scale.

A show that does this fantastically is *Unreal,* which I binged while house sitting for friends in their gorgeous house just out of Ōtaki several years ago. I identified strongly with the lead even though in many ways she's very different from me. It showcases the hidden underbelly of reality TV, the scheming that goes on. I loved it but it is too painful and drama filled to ever rewatch.

This is not the first book to deal with a dating show, nor is it the first based on *Pride and Prejudice*. Curtis Suttenfield's *Eligible* was part of the Austen project which attempted to recreate all of Austen's novels in a modern setting, her contribution to the project moved the furthest from the original. It's a shame the project was never completed, *Persuasion* and *Mansfield Park* proved too difficult to modernise perhaps.

As I completed my first draft of this novel *The Courtship* was screening in the USA. As I was working my way through edits it screened on TVNZ and I spoke about it on my podcast The Amateur Austenite, going slightly off form to build a whole season around the show. *The Courtship* attempts to create a dating show like *The Bachelorette* and mix in a regency setting. Unfortunately the "setting" becomes stage dressing rather quickly but I still adored it.

My dear friend Katherine, to whom I owe thanks for many things, suggested I read *The Charm Offensive* by Alison Cochrun which touched me deeply. I cried the entire second half of the book and read the whole thing in less than 16 hours. It explores the world of dating reality shows with a heavy slant towards the queer community, something that has always spoken to me and a voice that was getting louder as I wrote this book. I've always identified as bisexual but at almost 40 realised I'm asexual. You'll notice more representation here than in my previous works and *The Charm Offensive* is partly to thank, as is my own journey.

Thanks to those who sat beside me as I wrote; the Johnsonville writers group and Raewyn. To those who always encourage; Cassie, my mother, Katherine (as I said, I have a lot to thank her for), Pat, Sophia.

My beta readers and editor have helped polish the novel to be more cohesive, for this I thank you. The Writers Apothecary had the brilliant idea for the chapter and section titles.

About the Author

Frances lives in Wellington, New Zealand / Aotearoa and is of Ngati Porou and Te Whanau ā Apanui descent.

She does a lot of things: writing, running the Jane Austen Society of New Zealand / Aotearoa, hosting The Amateur Austenite podcast and facilitating "write with me" and "read with me" sessions online. If you want to get some writing done or have someone to discuss Austen with (or host a book club) check out her website francesduncandoes.com

www.ingramcontent.com/pod-product-compliance
Lightning Source LLC
Chambersburg PA
CBHW020334160726
47992CB00004B/1842

* 9 7 9 8 2 1 5 0 6 5 7 4 7 *